I0586693

THE NEON
HEART

THE SYNTHETIC ALBATROSS SERIES
BOOK TWO

The Neon Heart
AdventureWorldsPress.com

First Printing. April 2019

Published By
Adventure Worlds Press
Windsor Ontario

Printed in Canada.

ISBN 978-0-9949803-4-2 (paperback)

Cover by Christian Laforet
Author Photo by Khoa Nguyen

THE NEON HEART

BEN VAN DONGEN

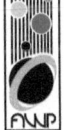

FOR MY NEPHEW
WHO SHOULDN'T READ THIS
FOR A FEW YEARS

ONE
LOOKING DOWN
ON THE EARTH

Reggie stood on the upper promenade and looked down at the Earth. The view slid past as the outer ring of the corporate-owned space station slowly revolved, the rotation creating gravity. Hanging from wires in front of the huge windows, the old International Space Station looked like it was still orbiting the planet. Reggie yawned, covering his mouth. He checked his wrist display. He'd been waiting two hours for his meeting with the Director of Amcoral, the second largest of the amalgamated corporate groups that controlled the planet and colonies.

His spot on the promenade rotated past the Earth and the shipyards came into view. Two massive Goliath Class transports were preparing for a deep space haul. Reggie leaned on the railing and peered at the ships. The bulbous forward section pointed away from him and tapered to a long cylinder. Around the middle was a huge spoke ring housing the Faster Than Light field generator, set much like the outer ring of the space station. The cylindrical center structure continued and flared out into the gigantic power plant and the conventional propulsion engine at the back.

A framework of girders and cables encased the slender middle sections and provided a place for platforms where workers and robots completed the construction. The tiny figures in environmental suits swarmed the ship like flies on the carcass of some strange, large animal. The second ship, identical to the first but free from its framework, was being prepared for departure. Reggie felt his heart beat harder as the conventional engines started to glow. He stared at the Goliath, trying to reconcile its actual size with its distance. He hadn't notice the woman who'd stopped next to him until she spoke.

"It's pretty amazing, huh." She shook out her long blond hair. It fell across her shoulders. Her jacket, black synthetic leather, had a large insignia of the biggest corporation, Telbak-Intercom, with dark blue stripes running behind it. She was a bit taller than he was, her heeled boots putting her over the top.

"Hi, Teal." Reggie shrugged his shoulders adjusting his own jacket—brown flex-teck with orange stripes behind the Amcoral logo. "What brings you to the enemy's station?"

Teal laughed so loudly she snorted. "Enemy. You're rich, you know that?"

Reggie scratched his head and turned back to the departing ship.

Teal punched him in the arm, harder than necessary. "I'm just teasing. I've been summoned. Amcoral called Telbak and asked for me specifically—apparently. What about you?"

"I work here," he said. The ship was passing the dock, heading into open space.

"You work for the company. A company that spans almost as many worlds as the one I work for. What are you doing here, on the station, on the top level of the promenade, outside the Director's office?"

"They have an extension for me."

Teal put her hand on his arm. "Wait, you are working off-contract right now?"

He cleared his throat and nodded.

"What the hell are you still doing here? Hasn't Telbak tried to get you back? Or, like, any other company?"

"Yeah."

The ship accelerated, but without reference, looked like it was hardly moving. Reggie knew it was going fast, and picking up speed rapidly. It appeared to shrink ever-so-slightly as it headed for the moon, but it would take hours to get there.

"They must have offered you a bundle. I had no idea you were that valuable a commodity." Teal chuckled with a snort.

"What do you want, Teal?"

"I'm just busting your balls." Teal leaned on her elbow, facing him. "Hey. Have you been off-contract before? I'm getting close to mine and I'm starting to get offers."

"This is, will be, my third extension. If I take it."

Teal took an exaggerated step back. "What? Third? What are you waiting for? You could have gotten a promotion by now, gotten into management."

"It's not for me."

She threw her head back and laughed. "You're a weird guy."

"I guess. Do you know what you're here for?"

Teal blew a strand of hair out of her face. "I have an idea. They asked me to put a team together. Some joint operation, so I assume it's either a Telbak holding and you guys have something we want or the other way around."

Reggie turned away from the departing ship and sighed. "Whatever they want, I'd better get a good offer because the payment for my last job just left the shipyards."

Teal nodded to the Goliath. "That one? Where's

it heading?"

"Gliese."

"What the hell is on Gliese? I thought Amcoral was pulling out." She grinned. "Pulling out."

Reggie chuckled, shaking his head. "Yeah. There is only one more transport to go." He nodded to the ship still under construction.

"Okay. But why?"

"Why go?" He raised his eyebrows. "It's far. It's different."

Teal put her hand on his shoulder again. "You are weird, man."

Reggie heard a beep and his comm-band vibrated. He pulled up his sleeve and turned his wrist to see the screen. The Director's assistant stared at him in the pale image.

The thin man sat rigid at his desk. "The Director is ready to see you. Please proceed to her office at once." The words were relayed to Reggie through the small circular pad stuck behind his right ear.

"Yeah." Reggie nodded. He shook his wrist, cutting off the image.

Teal grabbed his arm before he could pull his sleeve down. "See! This is what I'm talking about. Who still uses a comm-band? Even the savages Earth-Side have implants."

Reggie pulled free from her grip. "I don't want any corporate chips in my head. If you were smart, you wouldn't either."

Shaking her head, Teal turned back towards the departing ship. "Weird."

"If you say so." Reggie walked to the stairs behind them. They led up to the Director's office on its own level of the station. His comm-band buzzed again. He checked his wrist and Teal's face glared at him.

"You should say yes to the job. One last hurrah before you head into the wild black yonder and whatever you have waiting for you on Gliese."

Reggie stopped at the bottom of the stairs and looked back at Teal. "What are you doing?"

She was staring at a spot in space in front of her, at the image she saw from her implant. "If you say yes, I'll make your trip one of my conditions in the contract. I'm negotiating for Telbak."

"Why?" Reggie addressed Teal, not her image.

"Call it a favour for an old friend." She smiled. "Besides, maybe I know more about this mission than you do and I'd rather have you guiding my squad than some tourist who will get us all killed."

"What do you know?"

"You'll find out in a minute." Teal winked.

TWO
A THIRD
EXTENSION

The Director's assistant met Reggie at the top of the stairs. The thin man put his hand out to stop Reggie on the last step.

"I just have to perform a scan, sir." The assistant held out his hand and his pinky finger glowed. He swiped down to Reggie's legs then back up to his head.

"She's getting a little paranoid, isn't she?" Reggie raised an eyebrow.

The assistant made a *tsk* sound. "It's procedure. Besides, on a joint operation, you can never be too sure."

Reggie grinned. "Okay. Am I clear?"

Lowering his hand, the man stepped aside. "Yes. Though I see you still don't have an implant."

"Sure don't." Reggie went to the assistant's tall desk.

"They haven't made it a condition?"

"Not yet." Reggie nodded to the interior door. "She ready for me?"

"Not yet." Smirking, the assistant went to a table set up by the stairs. The only thing on it was a materializer—a symbol of the Director's importance. The machine was made in-house and not available for the public. It cost nearly as much to make as the Goliath ships Reggie was watching earlier, easily more than they had ever paid him for his services.

"May I offer you something to drink?" The assistant smiled.

"Can that thing make orange juice?" Reggie's mouth watered.

"It can make anything, sir." The assistant punched something in on the screen and the device hummed. A cup dropped into an open slot behind a plastic door. The sound increased and the materializer shook. Liquid poured into the cup. The device let out a ding and the shaking stopped. The assistant slid the door up and took the cup over to Reggie.

"Enjoy."

Reggie sniffed the liquid and sighed. Taking a sip, he smiled.

"Have you had orange juice before?"

"Yeah. It's been a long time."

The assistant's eyes glazed over as he stared at his personal projection. "The Director will see you now." He gestured to the door.

Reggie nodded. He walked up to the door and it opened for him automatically. The office was huge. The windows making up the back wall bowed inward, matching the interior curve of the station. The main room was roughly square and was set up in the style of old corporate offices of the twentieth century. Leather couches surrounded a coffee table near the middle of the space. Shelves lined one wall, and a big desk was near the windows, facing into the room. Two chairs were set in front of it and the Director was sitting behind it in a tall chair that swiveled and pivoted with her movements.

The space was warm on the otherwise cool station.

The Director stood. "Why don't we have an informal meeting?" She walked to one of the couches and sat.

Reggie nodded and took a seat across from her. The leather squeaked as he got comfortable. He put his drink down. The Director cleared her throat and he remembered to use one of the coasters on the table.

"I see you got something from the materializer."

"Yes. Thank you." Reggie raised his cup.

"I'm proud of that device. It will revolutionize many industries when we get it into production." The Director inclined her head.

"It makes good orange juice."

"That's right. You had a tree when you were a child?" The Director crossed her legs and leaned back.

"My family had a small one on the balcony."

"And, it was stolen?

"As things were. Director…"

"Please, Reginald. Call me Victoria."

"Victoria. I suspect this meeting isn't about the materializer."

Taking a deep breath, Victoria adjusted her jacket. It was fitted, broad at her shoulders and narrow at her midsection. It stopped short at her belt. Her emblem was pinned to the left shoulder and the Amcoral logo was set on her chest.

"Are you always so averse to pleasantries, Reginald?"

"Not always. But when my payment is halfway to the moon, I have bigger concerns than oranges."

Victoria pursed her lips. "I have a job for you."

"That's funny. You haven't paid me for the last contract and you want me to sign another one."

"You knew there would be complications when you asked for your last fee." Victoria leaned forward.

"I don't see what's so complicated about it. You deposit my credits into an account and save me a space on the next transport to Gliese. I signed the paperwork and did the job. You owe me."

"I need you for something before you go. It's important."

"Important enough to welch on the contract? I don't want to have to go to the Corporate Council." Reggie crossed his arms.

"Don't threaten me. It's tacky. Besides, the contract can only be fulfilled if the ship hasn't left. There is one transport to go. I can't guarantee I can get you there before it departs tomorrow." Victoria waved her hand and Reggie's comm-band pulsed.

He pulled up his sleeve and saw a copy of his contract with a passage highlighted.

"In such an event, we are within our rights as a corporate entity to provide compensation of equal value."

Reggie pulled his sleeve back down. "And what's that?"

"Five million credits—plus your accrued compensation. Should be nearly six million in total." Victoria smiled.

"That's insane. Managers don't make that much."

"This is an important mission. I'd gladly hand you the money if it would keep you here. I doubt the Council would see any problem with that amount."

Reggie sighed and looked out the window.

"Don't be so glum. There is a chance you can still make the last transport."

"What are the chances you won't pull the same stunt?" Reggie chewed on his cheek and thought about the Goliath in the dock.

"I am willing to put a clause in the contract stating that the only way we can offer you any payment other than the transportation to Gliese is if you don't make it back here on time."

"And what are you offering—for this last mission?"

"Land."

Reggie looked back at Victoria.

"Your choice of former Amcoral property on Gliese. Full ownership, no cost."

He narrowed his eyes.

"You won't get a better deal than that." Victoria leaned back. "And as for the transport under construction, it seems that I have put the shuttles on lockdown. Which means there is no way for you to sneak onto the ship before it leaves. Your only way on board is to take this mission."

"What is it?"

Victoria took a deep breath. "You aren't going to like it, but I need you to listen."

"Go on."

"We want you to go down to the surface, to the Wall, and retrieve a time travel device from the bottom level."

Reggie stood and stormed towards the door,

spilling the orange juice. A small, flat robot scurried from its place in the wall and zipped over to clean the spill, nearly tripping-up Reggie. He kicked at it, but it avoided his foot. "You're crazy, the Board is filled with morons, and I will be filing a complaint with the Council."

"Reggie, wait!"

Reggie paused at Victoria using the familiar of his name. He shook his head and went to the door. It didn't open.

"Let me out!"

"Please listen."

"Time travel is impossible, the Wall is a backwards, savage, shithole within a bigger shithole city on a shithole planet, and getting to the lowest floor is suicide. What else is there?"

"The Board doesn't believe in time travel, but it is in their best interest to prove it false. The last time something impossible was dismissed, the Espers were discovered—in the Wall, mind you."

"I know that, Victoria. I was there."

"Your brother—"

"My brother had his head scooped out by a gang of primitive thugs who thought if they ate his brain, they could get his powers. So, don't start lecturing me about the Wall or about Espers. It's tacky." Reggie stomped halfway back to Victoria, turned back to the door, stopped, and turned back to her. "That's why Teal is here. Telbak owns the Wall so it's a joint operation. She knew the whole time. That dirty—"

"Reggie. Please consider the offer. You could claim the Gliese headquarters. That's nearly a full block and five stories. It's the most expensive building on the planet. We need someone who knows the Wall, someone who has been underground. You bring Teal and her squad to the bottom floor, find the machine, the"—Victoria checked her projection—"'The Neon Heart', and bring it back here. If you can't, just confirm it doesn't work and destroy any evidence and I promise you I will get you on the last ship to Gliese."

"The Neon Heart is a place. It's what passes for a bar that far down."

"There you go. Right there. That's why we need you. There isn't a single operative in Amcoral or Telbak who knows the Wall like you do." Victoria stood and went over to him. "Please, Reggie. Think this through."

Reggie sighed and ran his hand through his short hair. "You made me a promise before, Victoria. You promised me I would never have to go to the Wall ever again."

The Director looked away. She made a motion with her hand and Reggie's comm-band buzzed.

"That's the contract. A ship is waiting. Teal and her squad will be there."

"With an Esper mind-reader?"

"Two, but we have someone to go with you. Someone with a unique ability."

"I don't like people getting inside my head."

"It's standard protocol when going to the surface, to protect from wild readers. But like I said. We have someone who can help you."

"Another Esper?"

"So much more. She has an ability, but it's not just reading minds."

Reggie slumped his shoulders. "Not telekinesis?"

Victoria stood rigid. "No. We still have no one proven to move things, but she can block others from reading minds."

"What?" Reggie squinted.

"I've seen her in action. You can imagine how valuable she is to the company."

"And you're sending her with me into the Wall?"

Victoria reached out her hand, but stopped. "I made sure it was part of the deal. I told you I'd look out for you when I sent you on your first assignment, back when I was an administrator. As the Director, I can't keep every promise I've made in my career, but I meant that when I said it."

"Do you mean it? You will hold the transport for me?"

"I can hold it for twenty-four hours."

Reggie checked the contract still displayed on his

wrist. "And you are going to keep this promise? You and the Board aren't going to back out on this contract?"

"Here." A new message appeared over the contract displayed on Reggie's arm. It was a live feed of the conversation he was having with the Director. "When you leave this office, the recording will stop and be saved to your profile. You can use it with the Council if I back out. It may not get you to Gliese if the ship is gone, but it will definitely mean my job and likely a few of the Amcoral Board members, too."

Reggie closed his eyes. He pictured the Goliath still in the framework, the final stage of construction coming to a close. He balled his hands into fists. "I'm counting on you, Victoria."

"I'm the one counting on you."

THREE
MISSION
PARAMETRES

Reggie marked his bio-signature on the contract and left the office. He started a timer on his comm-band counting down the twenty-four hours. Ignoring the assistant, he went down the stairs. Teal was waiting for him at the bottom.

"So. Do I call my team and start prepping the drop ship?" She fell into step with him as he stiffly walked down the promenade to the lifts.

"How long have you known?" He didn't look at her.

"They came to me first since the Wall is a Telbak holding. Because this thing was an Amcoral find and they wanted a joint operation, I suggested you."

Reggie stopped, turned to Teal, pointed his finger at her, shook his head then continued, stomping down the hall.

Teal caught up. "Victoria already insisted it had

to be you. My opinion really doesn't matter when it comes to directors negotiating a mission."

"You couldn't have told them that I won't go back there?"

"It's not all about you. If I have to go, I want someone I can rely on. I trust you as an operative and no one else knows as much about the Wall." Teal pulled her hair behind an ear and skipped to match his gait.

Reggie looked at her out of the corner of his eye. "I'm not happy, Teal. I was supposed to be on that ship and now they are holding me hostage."

"I'm not responsible for that."

"Do you know what they are sending us in to find?"

Teal chuckled. "Yeah. Pretty ridiculous."

Reggie waved his arms. "It's insane. We are probably going to die trying to get this thing."

"No. You've got something up your sleeve," Teal said.

"What?" Reggie stopped again. Teal overshot and shuffled back.

"You were born in the Wall and you worked there for your first whole bunch of years. You know more about it than the experts either of our companies hire. You have some way down there that they don't even know exists. I'd bet my wage on it."

"I ought to deny that just to see you lose." Reggie stared at her, frowning. She smirked, making him crack a smile. "Come on. I'm still upset."

"But I'm right," Teal said in a sing-song tone. "You can't stay mad at meeeee."

"I sure can. Is your crew standing by?" Reggie went up to the bank of elevators and pressed his thumb to a scanner. The numbers over the door turned green and counted up to their current floor.

"Yeah. I've got a pretty good squad. They know how to shoot and they take orders well. It's a package deal, though. You get all three or none of them."

"And Espers?"

"One of the soldiers is trained, and I've got a hotshot with a bad attitude and a great record. I told them to leave you be. The soldier will but the hotshot is a bit of a prick." Teal put her hands on her hips.

"Apparently Amcoral has someone for me for just that contingency." Reggie raised an eyebrow.

"Oooh." Teal matched his expression. "I've heard something about that. Some kind of blocker your guys found and snatched up from a colony before anyone else got a chance."

"I'll believe it when I see it."

"Well, if there are people who can read someone's thoughts, why can't there be someone who can block them? That's just nature, dude."

Reggie crossed his arms. "I retain a healthy skep-

19

ticism."

The elevator dinged and the doors whooshed open. They stepped inside. Reggie pressed the button for the drop ship bays and staging area on the Earth-facing end of the station. The panel next to the buttons blinked, asking for his thumbprint again.

The elevator descended, losing gravity as it slipped out of the ring and along the spoke to the center wheel. Reggie held onto a bar set into the wall, but Teal floated to the middle and did somersaults. Her hair flowed out like it was alive, and snapped after her as she spun.

"That's going to hurt if you get caught when the gravity kicks in."

Teal stuck a foot out to stop so she was facing Reggie, but upside-down. "You are entirely no fun."

"I am aware and perfectly fine with that."

As the car moved into the inner ring, Teal expertly righted herself. Her feet touched down and her hair cascaded around her face. She pulled it back and winked. "I'm going to get you to loosen up one of these days."

"Not unless you find a way to Gliese."

Teal punched him in the arm. "So, I've got until we're done this mission."

The elevator stopped and they got out. The inner ring was much smaller, making the curvature overt and, since it spun in conjunction with the outer ring, it produced less centripetal force. Teal bounced as she walked, exaggerating her movements. Reggie tried to keep the same angry stride as on the promenade, but the lower gravity made his movements unstable. He settled with little hops on each step.

"I know it's a joint mission, but I've got command on this one," Reggie said.

Teal dropped her shoulders. "Fine. I'll pretend you are in charge."

"I'm not getting into it again, Teal. A mission needs one person giving the orders. You know I'll take your input and let you boss your squad around, but when the shit hits the fan, they'll have to look to one individual to take charge."

"It's not my fault you don't use your resources effectively."

Reggie clenched his jaw.

"I know, relax." She shoved him, sending him careening in the low gravity.

"Teal."

"Sorry. I didn't mean that." She put up her hands. "I know the Wall is dangerous. I'll be professional when it matters. But you need to loosen up."

Reggie grimaced.

"Or not. Jeez." Teal shrugged. "I will happily give you command."

"Thank you."

"You know, it's a little insulting that you don't

think I know this stuff. I may not have the experience on Earth, but I run plenty of my own missions. I know how to second and I have no problem giving up command when it's the right thing to do."

Reggie sighed. "Sorry. I'm just—" He pursed his lips. "I'm not looking forward to this."

"Real talk." She stopped him. "I know this is a bogus deal and I get that this mission is stupid. I can even get why you have no interest in going down there, the tremendous danger aside. I'm on your side in this. We go down, make as little noise as possible, and get the hell out."

"Thanks." Reggie nodded.

"Now, let's go meet the kids."

FOUR
THE
STAGING AREA

The mission staging areas were set around the docking bays in the center hub of the station. Half the ring was reserved for the countless missions Amcoral was involved with across explored space. The other was for loading and unloading goods.

Reggie led the way into a locker room adjacent to his mission's assigned staging area. Teal followed. Her expression was severe, her jovial nature gone. Three soldiers, two women and an older man, were putting on their gear, checking each other over for proper fit. The man had salt and pepper hair shaved close on the sides and in a bun on top of his head. A scar ran from his hairline down his forehead.

The woman fixing the carbon plates running along his spine was much younger and half his size. Her pink, green, and blue hair was in a tight ponytail. She grunted, her lip curling, as she pulled at the small pieces on her partner's suit. The third soldier, strapping on her chest plate, was taller, but thinner than the other woman. She looked up at Reggie as he entered and furrowed her brow. Inhaling sharply, she went back to affixing her armor. As Telbak soldiers, their armor was dark blue and black with silver accents, like Teal's patch.

A man sat on the adjacent bench. He wore a similar jacket to Teal, but it went to his knees. His close-cropped hair was styled like a manager, professional and stiff. He wore heavy makeup with dark blue lipstick and silver eyeliner. Tilting his head to the side, he stared at Reggie, unblinking.

"So, you're the guy who knows the Wall?" His mouth turned down slightly looking like an alien slug under the blue makeup.

Teal stepped in front of Reggie and pointed at the man. "What did I tell you, Dollard?"

"I don't need to read his mind to know that little tidbit."

"Know that little tidbit, what?" Teal put her hand to her ear.

"Commander." Dollard frowned and looked away.

"Better, but the commander for this mission is going to be Reggie here." Teal pointed over her shoulder with a thumb. "He's got the intel and he's got the lead. I'm second and Azikiwe?"

The slender woman working on her chest plate looked up.

"You're third, got it?"

She nodded, dark bangs falling over her eyes. "Yes, ma'am."

Reggie took a deep breath and peered at Teal from the side.

She nodded and stepped in line next to him.

Reggie checked his comm-band for the mission briefing. He scanned down the document to the list of personnel. "Where is Emerson?"

A woman, younger than the soldiers, stepped around a bank of lockers in the middle of the room. "Here."

She wore a stiff Amcoral jacket, bright orange with a huge logo that went from the front, around one sleeve, and disappeared to the back. It was a size too large, making her thin legs look even smaller. Her brown hair was long and tucked into the back of the jacket.

"Right." Reggie cleared his throat. "I'm sure you've all been briefed, and if you were chosen by Teal, I have every confidence in you. The mission is deceptively simple. We are to head planet-side to the Eastern Urban Sprawl to the complex known as the Wall." Reggie shot a glance at Dollard. The Esper wasn't looking.

"We'll be descending to the bottom floor to a

25

place called The Neon Heart."

The old soldier cut in. "I thought the item was the Heart?"

Teal frowned at him.

He blushed and put up his hand. "Sorry."

"It's fine." Reggie shook his head. "I'm not sure if the item is also named the Heart, or if the information Amcoral got was incomplete, but at the bottom level of the Wall is an establishment, a bar that deals in everything and anything deemed immoral or illegal. It's called The Neon Heart. Supposedly, that is where the item is located. Either way, that's where we'll be looking for it. If it is there, we are to secure it and bring it back with us to the station. It will be handed over to a team comprised of engineers and scientists from both our companies. If we can't take it with us, we verify it's a fake and destroy it, and anything related to it."

Reggie scanned the room. "Any questions so far?" No one moved. Emerson had her eyes shut tightly. Her face was scrunched and she shook slightly.

"Okay. I want to say one more thing and I want you to take it very seriously. You have all heard of the Wall, I'm sure." The group nodded, except for Dollard. "You may have been told how dangerous it is, that underground there are a bunch of inhuman monsters who will eat you. The reality is very much worse than that. This whole thing is stupid and going down with anything less than an entire battalion is suicide. But, they want this thing kept as quiet as possible. So, we are what we've got."

Reggie sighed. "If we keep our heads, don't do anything foolish, and shoot anything that looks remotely hostile, we should be able to get out of this with minor injuries." Crossing his arms, Reggie stared at Dollard. "You may think I am exaggerating. I am not." He glanced at the soldiers. "I want as few casualties as possible, so stay alert, stay focused, and avoid any unnecessary curiosity. There are some weird things down there. Just leave them be."

The old soldier raised his hand again.

Reggie pointed to him. "Yes?"

"Muller, sir." He put his hand down. "Do you think it's real?"

"No." Reggie shook his head, his keeping face placid.

The woman who had been working on her own armor raised her hand. "Then why are we going?"

"Azikiwe, right?"

"Yes, sir."

Reggie scratched his head. "We are going because the possibility of it existing is too much for our companies to ignore. Does that answer your question?"

"Yes, sir." Azikiwe nodded and went back to

suiting up.

Reggie went up to the third soldier. She stood as he approached.

"At ease." Reggie waved his hand and she relaxed. "What's your name?"

"Hoa, sir."

"You're the third Esper?" he asked.

"Third? I thought there was only two of us."

"The girl," Reggie nodded towards Emerson who was holding her arm and scuffing her boot on the floor, "She's got some new ability."

"Blocking?" Hoa's eyes widened.

Reggie smiled. "Yeah. You feel it?"

"Yes, sir. It's like there is a wall around her, and you." Hoa stiffened. "Not that I tried to read you, sir. I am under strict orders."

Reggie put his hand out. "It's okay. I believe you. It's nice to know it's real."

"It makes it harder to sense others. I mean, it's like a distraction or something," Hoa said.

"It probably sticks out like a sore thumb to Espers, too." He bit his lip.

Hoa looked up at him. "Yeah. I hadn't thought of that."

"Still, could be helpful. Some of the Espers in the Wall have some wild power." Reggie clapped her on her shoulder plate. "See you in the staging area."

"Sir." Hoa nodded and continued to help Muller.

Reggie bypassed Dollard and went over to Emerson. Teal had made her way to the girl and was trying to engage her in chitchat.

"How are you, kid?"

Teal raised an eyebrow. "Me? Her? You've got to be more specific, old man."

"Her."

Emerson stuffed her hands in the pockets of her oversized jacket. "I'm fine, and don't call me kid."

"Sorry." Reggie took a deep breath. "Looked like you were struggling with something while I was giving my little speech."

"Little?" Teal put her hands on her hips. Reggie glared at her and she took a step back.

Emerson looked away. "That guy was trying to read you."

"Looked uncomfortable," Reggie said.

"It's my job."

"How old are you?" Reggie furrowed his brow.

"Why?" Emerson avoided looking at him.

"Because we are about to do something stupid, and not the fun stupid that kids your age should be doing."

Emerson snapped her head to face him. "I'm not a kid. I'm an Amcoral employee and my mission is to stick with you and protect you."

Reggie rubbed his chin. "Okay. Not a kid. Still, you can't be older than seventeen."

"I'm twenty. Not that it matters."

Teal put her hand on Reggie's shoulder. "Give her a break. We were younger than that when we started."

Reggie turned to her. "Yeah, but we didn't go into the Wall for our first mission." He looked back at Emerson. "I appreciate that the Director assigned you to watch my back, but I'm making a call as mission commander."

"You can't take me off the mission!" Emerson leaned towards him, face scrunched. The rest of the squad froze.

"Come here." Reggie stepped around the lockers in the middle of the room and sat on a bench. "Have a seat."

Emerson flopped down onto the bench, her jaw tight.

"Tell me what's going on."

"What's going on is you're trying to take me off the mission."

Reggie shrugged. "I am."

"It's not fair." Emerson crossed her arms.

"I'm trying to keep you from going on a suicide mission." Reggie pointed to the soldiers on the far side of the lockers. "Those people signed up to risk their lives. Even the Esper knows how dangerous this is. I'm not convinced you do."

Emerson opened her mouth but Reggie put up

a hand.

"I'm not done." He sighed. "I need you to realize that there is a good chance that some of us are going to die on this mission. We will very likely have to kill a number of people in the Wall and they will all be trying to kill us. Out of the seven going, we will be lucky if only one of us dies. And the people down there, if you can call them people, they won't just shoot us and be done with it. They make it last. They'll torture you, they'll eat you, they'll…"

Reggie shook his head.

Teal sat on the bench. "He's not exaggerating." She put her arm around Emerson. "Were you given a cyanide pill?"

The girl nodded.

"It's for this kind of mission."

Reggie grimaced. "I'm trying really hard not to treat you like a child, but I wouldn't forgive myself if I dragged you into my mess. I'm trying to give you an out."

"I don't want it." Emerson sneered.

Teal stood and guided Reggie a few steps away. "You gave it a shot. Now you're just getting her riled up. If you keep pushing it she may end up doing something stupid to prove some dumb-ass point."

Reggie tipped his head to the side. "Why?"

"You're an older male in charge of her first mission. She's scared and has something to prove. Besides, you don't know what Victoria may be holding over her."

Reggie shook his head. "Okay." He looked over to Emerson who was picking at the wooden bench with a fingernail. "Fine. You win. On one condition."

"What?" The girl looked away.

"When we are down there, you stick next to me or Teal like you're on a tether." Reggie glanced at Teal, then back to Emerson. "If we both die, Azikiwe is next in charge."

The girl eyed him, mouth open.

"Well?"

She nodded and looked away again.

"Okay. Well, you'd better get yourself squared away. We have to get prepped for the drop."

She sighed. "I don't know what to do."

Teal stepped in front of Reggie, preemptively cutting him off. "That's fine." She glanced at Reggie. "It's fine. I'll help while the mean old man worries about himself for a minute."

Reggie turned and walked to a door to the side of the room. "You're not funny, Teal."

"Oh, I'm hilarious."

FIVE
SHINY AND NEW

The door led to a private room for mission commanders. A single locker was already stocked with his requested equipment. He had to use his thumbprint to access it. A screen on the wall, split into four sections, showed two views of the team in the adjacent locker room, the shuttle bay, and an orbital shot of his target location. From the satellite, the Wall looked like a city-sized barricade cutting across the middle of the Eastern Urban District. Skyscrapers were dotted around it like pinpoints. Impressive monoliths of nano-carbon, graphene, and reinforced glass seemed insignificant to the Great Wall keeping them separated.

Reggie gritted his teeth and checked on the squad. The soldiers were geared up, looking over their rifles. Dollard was sitting cross-legged like a monk, and Teal was helping Emerson with an armored vest. Without her big coat, the girl looked taller, but still so young.

With a huff, Reggie went to his own equipment. A new jacket was hanging on the hook in the locker. It was bright orange, like the girl's, but made of flex-teck, like his old one. When he touched it, the material rippled and changed colour to match the grey of the locker. Reggie blinked and rubbed the material. It felt the same as his, but almost faded away into the space around it. A note was stuck to the front of it in the Director's handwriting that just said 'check the pocket.'

Reggie reached inside and pulled out a small wooden case. Opening the lid, he saw a new comm-band, a bone-conducting speaker and microphone patch for behind his ear, and a smaller plastic contact-lens case. Taking off his old equipment, he placed it in the box, putting the replacements on. As soon as the patch was stuck behind his ear, a message from the Director played.

"Just a little thank you I cooked up in my materializer. The jacket is some new tech hitting the market soon, but I had to make the band and earpiece custom. I still think you're a baby for not just getting an implant, but I owe you, so I'll placate you. They are as up to date as the tech can get. They won't be as fast as an implant, but they have almost all the bells and whistles. Which brings me to the bonus item."

Reggie opened the case for the contacts. Sitting in the circular compartments were nearly invisible discs of plastic. He could just make out the traces of circuitry on them in copper and gold.

"You've got to put them on to continue the message. It can be a little unnerving if you haven't worn contacts before, but they used to be common back when I was running ops. Just pull down your bottom eyelid and pop them in. You're going to want to blink a bunch and rub your eyes. Blink all you like, but don't touch. The lenses will slip into place and the whole system will connect."

Taking a deep breath, Reggie took the case to the mirror over a sink on the wall. He looked at himself in the mirror and scratched his head. Grimacing, he touched the first lens. It stuck to his finger. He groaned as he brought it to his eye. Once it was in, he blinked furiously, as the Director had said, and it slipped into place. The view in the one eye was slightly tinted. He couldn't see the minute electronics, but it added a haze of yellow, making the room seem brighter. The effect on half his vision made him shut the afflicted eye.

"One more." He shuddered. "Good thing I got a private room for this." Repeating the process, complete with the disgust, he got the second lens into position. His comm-band vibrated once and the patch behind his ear sent a single ping of sound along his skull to his inner ear.

The Director appeared in a window floating in front of him. "Took you long enough."

Reggie spun around and the image stayed with him, floating over the background of the locker room. "Whoa."

"This is what you've been missing all these years, on-the-fly information in a heads-up display. Watch this." The image shrunk to a small box in the upper right of his vision and became transparent, letting the background show through. On the bottom left a status of his crew appeared. It was large, showing their heartbeats, and a postage-stamp view of what they saw. Above that was a map of the lockers and hangar with everyone's position. He caught himself in the mirror and above his reflection his personal info popped into view.

"That's not even the best part." The Director waved a hand and the boxes faded in and out, changed size and shape, and moved around Reggie's view. It made his head spin and he shut his eyes, but the show continued with a black backdrop.

"Stop!" Reggie put his hand out and the boxes froze in place.

"Okay. A little much all at once," the Director said.

"Wait. Is that you?" Reggie opened his eyes. He

focused on the Director and her image grew to dominate his vision.

"Yes."

"But like, really you, now, in your office and not a recording."

"Of course." She grinned.

"Then can you make this stop? I'm going to be sick."

She chuckled. "You can override me at any time. I'm not some sadistic monster. You should be able to control it with your eyes, but that will take time. For now, the comm-band can track your hand movements and control the contacts accordingly."

Reggie reached out and swiped away the other boxes as if they were windows on a screen, and they disappeared beyond his view. "This is going to take some getting used to."

"You'll get there in no time. This is basically the same setup we used before the implants took over. It's less elegant, but you have your qualms."

"Thank you." Reggie touched the tiny pad behind his ear. "For, uh. Everything, I guess."

"You're welcome. It's rather selfishly motivated, though. I need you to succeed, so providing you with the equipment to make that happen is common sense." She smiled. "You'd better get going. Time is of the essence and your squad will be waiting for you."

A timer appeared in the bottom right corner of Reggie's vision. It had already been an hour since he'd left the Director's office, leaving twenty-three more to go before his last chance at Gliese flew off without him.

"Okay." Reggie nodded and slipped off his old jacket, hanging it in the locker. "Can I…"

"I'll have your old equipment ready for you at the shuttle when you're done."

Reggie slipped the new one on, but stopped, pulling it over his shoulder. "You're not going to watch me the whole time, are you?"

The Director pursed her lips. "I have better things to do than monitor your entire operation. I do have a company to run. Besides, once you are in the Wall, communication will be compromised."

"Wish me luck." Reggie finished getting the jacket on, grabbed his pistol from the locker, and shut the door.

SIX
LONG WAY
DOWN

Before Reggie joined the others in the staging area, he checked out his new jacket. It seemed to have the same cut and bullet resistant properties as his old one, but the camouflage was something he'd only seen on high-end spec-ops gear. It must have cost the Director a fortune to produce, even with the materializer. Thankfully, he found he could sync the fabric to his comm-band and keep it from constantly trying to mimic its surroundings. The effect would draw attention if always on, defeating the purpose. He kept it orange, the apparent default colour, and set the camouflage to be pressure sensitive. He made sure his gun was securely holstered inside the jacket, and went into the staging area through a private door.

The open room was designed for large squads and divisions, so the small group looked awkward standing by the wall, their small pile of equipment next to them.

The soldiers stood at attention when Reggie walked in. Emerson, who had been leaning against the wall, pushed away from it. She looked to Teal who put a hand on her shoulder and whispered something to the girl. Dollard sat by himself on the floor, his bag on his lap. He didn't look as Reggie joined them.

"Okay. I've already given the speech, so if we're ready, let's get to the shuttle." Reggie gestured over his shoulder with a thumb. The soldiers grabbed their duffle bags and stiffly walked to the craft docked along the opposing wall.

Dollard sighed and didn't move.

Teal whooped, startling everyone. "Looking good, Captain. Let's go get 'em!" She hooked her arm around Emerson and led the girl to the ship behind the troops.

Reggie stood next to the remaining squad member. "Let's go, Dollard."

The man didn't look up. "I'm not finished preparing for our little journey."

Reggie clenched and unclenched his jaw. "Right. What do you need?"

"Some blasted peace and quiet for one."

Reggie gritted his teeth. "We'll be on the shuttle doing preflight. You have until then or I leave you behind and you lose out on your share."

Dollard snapped his head up to glare at him. The Esper had a scowl dug across his face. "You will do no such thing or you'll find Amcoral will be in breach of my contract. Besides, you wouldn't last one minute down there without me."

Reggie smirked. "First off, I couldn't care less about your contract. This is my last job. Screw Amcoral. Secondly, you seem more like a liability to me at this point. So, get your ass on board before pre-flight is done, or you can argue your case with the Council."

Leaving Dollard on the floor, Reggie went to the shuttle and climbed through the side hatch. The ship was a small orbital jumper, designed to take operatives and troops from the various space stations to Earth and back. The group fit comfortably with half a dozen empty spots to spare. The seats ran along the walls, leaving the middle open for squads to exit the aft ramp.

Reggie grabbed the back of the co-pilot's chair and scanned the cabin. Muller, Hoa, and Azikiwe were securing their bags and Emerson sat, her knees to her chest. Reggie went over to her. "Have you been in a shuttle before?"

"Yes," she said, looking down.

"Then you know you'll need to strap in."

The girl huffed, putting her feet down. She

grabbed the shoulder straps and slipped them over the big coat. Teal finished securing her duffle bag and slipped past them on her way to the cockpit. She made finger guns at Emerson and slapped Reggie on the ass. The soldiers found seats next to each other and pulled their harnesses on. Azikiwe grabbed Reggie's wrist, stopping him.

"Commander. As squad leader, I hope you can trust me to give autonomous orders to my troops—"

Reggie cut her off with a raised hand. "You are squad leader of three soldiers, Azikiwe. I'm not worried about stepping on your toes because I can assure you that I will. If we find ourselves in a tight spot and I start giving your soldiers direct orders, you're going to have to suck it up."

The woman glowered, her dark skin pulling tightly across his face.

Reggie let a sigh slip. "That being said. I am going to count on you to keep things running smoothly for the majority of the time. I don't want to cause any undue tension. I just want to get the job done and get as many of you back here alive as I can. Okay?"

Azikiwe nodded. "Yes, sir."

"Good." Reggie scanned the group, looking them each in the face, daring them to raise more objections. The soldiers stared at him. Emerson looked away, her knuckles already white from gripping the straps.

Reggie nodded again and went to the front of the shuttle. He strapped himself into the co-pilot's seat next to Teal who was flicking switches, readying the shuttle for departure.

"The kids all strapped in?" She smiled, looking at him out of the side of her eye.

"I thought you'd be the most childish."

She punched his shoulder. "I'm charming as shit. They're… I don't even know."

"Fragile. And mister big stuff isn't even on board yet."

"Dollard? He's a pain, but he's good. I've been in a tough spot with him and he came through." Teal focused on her personal, invisible screen, typing on an imaginary keyboard.

"If you say so." Reggie tried his own screen, displayed on the contact lenses sitting on his eyes. He managed to get a set of monitors to display, one of the cabin with the squad seated, one of the hangar, Dollard still sitting by himself, and a larger section showing what Teal was doing. "What's our launch time?"

"We've got an open window thanks to the Director. I'm just warming up the engines and waiting for Dollard."

"Can we just leave him behind?" Reggie crossed

his arms.

"There'd be hell to pay."

"I'll be on a ship to another solar system. Or dead in the Wall." He shrugged.

Teal twisted her mouth in thought. "Then I'd have to deal with it. Besides, he's good at what he does. Might be better off just to give him this pout and suck it up."

"I get the feeling I'll be doing a lot of that with this group."

"Just until we land. The reality should set them straight."

Reggie turned to face Teal. "Right. Light it up. I'm on a timeline." He looked to the back of the shuttle as much as he could while strapped in. "Everyone settled?"

Azikiwe responded, "Just waiting on Dollard, sir."

Reggie shook his head and connected to Dollard over the radio. Before he spoke, he chewed on his lip and glanced up, composing himself. "Dollard, you ready to go, we have a window."

"You just interrupted my meditation. I'm going to have to start all over again."

Reggie saw Dollard over the monitor in the corner of his view. He looked over to Teal, keeping the connection to Dollard open. "Button it up. Let's go to Earth."

Teal rolled her eyes and hit the button to close and seal the door. "Yes, sir."

Dollard got to his feet and ran for the shuttle. He ducked under the lowering door, landing on the floor.

"Nice of you to join us. Find your seat. We'll be moving in a moment." Reggie didn't bother to look back. He closed off the monitor to the staging area and the one showing the back of the ship grew to take its place.

Dollard stood and went to the last pair of seats at the back. "I'm going to report this to the Director and the Council."

The door shut and pressurized with a short puff of air and Teal pulled them away from the dock. The rest of the station was quiet. The normal traffic, shuttles coming and going constantly, was on hold to give them a clear shot out of the docking area and into the designated lane to Earth.

They eased out of the station, a speck in the huge open hangar that normally dealt with dozens of different-sized vessels simultaneously. The Earth loomed in front of them, taking up their entire view. Rings of satellites and debris cluttered their path, but buoys marked the safe routes. Ships flew to and away from the planet in constant streams. They joined a lineup heading to Earth and left the station behind.

THE NEON HEART

SEVEN
PLANET FALL

The shuttle shook as it hit air. Emerson let out a yelp that cut through the roar. Reggie saw her in his monitor. Her fingers clenched the straps of the harness—her eyes shut tightly. The soldiers were relaxed, focused. They knew their job, had ridden the atmosphere of dozens of planets. Heading to Earth was old hat. Dollard was passive. If the rough ride affected him, he didn't show it. His brow was still creased and the scowl on his face seemed permanent. Reggie thought about their altercation on the station and frowned. He needed to bury the hatchet or he'd have to deal with that conflict as well as the physical threats in the Wall.

He sighed.

Teal glanced at him. Her arms shook as she fought the atmosphere slamming against the ship, keeping them on course.

The view from the cockpit cleared as they slowed and he saw the city. There were dozens of massive urban sectors spread across the planet, made up of the continued expanse of the old cities converging. They grew like mold on fruit. Dense patches spread out into thin, searching tendrils—reaching towards each other. Out of all of them, the Eastern Urban Sprawl was among the largest. The skyscrapers, as big as the monolith ships stood on their end, seemed to rise up to meet them.

Teal leveled off the shuttle, joining the regular traffic like a beetle getting in the middle of a line of ants. She transmitted their landing instructions to the automated defenses of the Wall as the smaller, planetary ships veered away from the crag cutting the city in two.

"Where are we setting down?" Reggie pulled against his harness, looking over the nose of the shuttle to the ramshackle top level of the Wall.

"There is a landing pad, well, it's kind of like a landing pad. Really, it's just a reinforced roof—if you can call it reinforced." Teal left one hand on the controls and waved the other around for emphasis.

"The point?" Reggie put his hand on hers, stopping the motion.

"Right, the roof that stands a couple levels over the rest in that section over there." Teal pointed to a platform built on top of an old brick building like a graduation cap slipping to the side. Sitting on opposite corners of the landing pad, two turrets spun to face them, then rotated back towards the rest of the Wall, as if they had spotted the incoming target before getting the shuttle's authorization, and decided to look for other threats.

Reggie squinted at the building and his new contact lenses highlighted the platform, pointing out the obvious structural issues. "You're sure about that?"

"It'll be fine." Teal smiled and looked away.

Hoa yelled from the back, "She doesn't believe that."

"Hey!" Teal turned to face her. "No reading my mind, missy."

"I've got orders to stay out of his head. Yours is fair game."

Reggie turned Teal to face the windows. "Focus. I don't need an Esper to know that you're full of it. Just put us down—gently."

Teal went back to piloting the shuttle. She sat up in her seat, reading the monitors created by her implants, that only she could see. "Hey. I'm picking up someone in that building."

"Is that strange?" Reggie brought up the ship's scanners on his lenses.

"Up that high, yeah. It's supposed to be off limits. Telbak authorization only."

Reggie spotted the outline of a person in the

upper floors. He was thin, but the scanner picked up an old revolver and a black market implant. He set the scanner to check the platform. "He may be up to something. Be ready."

Azikiwe let out a 'hup' of acknowledgement and Reggie heard the soldiers unstrap and go to their stored equipment.

"I'm picking up something," Dollard added.

In his view of the cabin, Reggie saw Dollard scrunching his face like he was constipated. "From here?"

"It's just some surface emotions. He's nervous, scared of something."

"Should be scared of us," Azikiwe said.

"It's not that," said Dollard. "It's almost primal. I don't think it has anything to do with us."

Reggie nodded. "Okay. Stay on alert. Let's see what he does."

Teal brought them over the landing platform. "Scans are clear. No surprises."

"Set us down." Reggie unstrapped and went to the back. The soldiers were armed and in position to rush out the ramp as soon as they landed. Dollard was still focused on his reading, and Emerson stared at the floor. She was pale and looked like she was concentrating on keeping down her last meal. Reggie grabbed the bar running above the seats to steady himself as they landed.

"Dollard. Getting anything?"

"He's… He's frightened, like a rabbit. He's about to flee."

"He's running," Teal yelled from the front.

Reggie rubbed his chin. "Good work. Keep reading him as long as he's in range."

"That's what I'm doing." Dollard grimaced, peering at him though one open eye.

"Hell of a range." Reggie left the Esper and crouched next to Emerson as the engines whined down. "You still with us?"

She nodded, looking at her lap.

"The ride's a bit rough, but you'll get used to it. We're on the ground now."

"So to speak." Teal stepped up next to him. She looked to the soldiers and bumped him with her hip. He nodded and left her with the girl.

Reggie slipped behind the small squad. "Azikiwe, simple pattern, don't stray too far. Just make sure he's good and gone."

"Hup."

Reggie hit the release and the ramp dropped with a whoosh, stopping just before hitting the platform. The soldiers slipped out, scanning over the tops of their rifles as they went. They headed for the stairwell enclosure at the edge of the platform that led to the lower levels of the building.

Teal stepped beside him with Emerson under

her arm. "Whaddya say, Captain? All clear?"

"Let's see." Reggie walked down the ramp calmly, checking out the surroundings. When he reached the platform he turned to look back at the women. "Looks good to me. Chances are the landing scared most of the nearby rats from their nests anyway."

Reggie walked to the edge, surveying the surrounding buildings, getting his bearings. He brought up a window to see the status of the soldiers in the corner of his lens. Their vitals were steady, like their nerves. He contacted Azikiwe through his commband. "How's it looking?"

"Quiet. We stormed the first few floors, but he ran."

"That's good. Hold position by the stairwell. We're coming down."

"Do you want us to join you, sir?"

Waving the idea way, Reggie turned back to the shuttle. "No need. Area's clear. We'll be there momentarily."

Cutting the call, Reggie watched Teal skip down the ramp, Emerson dragged along, their arms interlocked. The girl looked like she was fighting a smile. He grinned himself and walked past them, into the shuttle. Dollard was still concentrating.

"Anything worth sharing?"

The Esper looked up. "No. He's getting out

of my range. Went right for the nearest exit."

"To the Wall?"

Dollard nodded.

"Well, let him go. We have the rest of this place to worry about."

THE NEON HEART

EIGHT
EARTH IS A
SHITHOLE

With their equipment in hand, Reggie sealed the shuttle, keying it to only open for one of their signatures. "Teal, you sure this pad is secure?"

Teal stood at the bottom of the ramp with Emerson. "I doubt anyone is getting past the turrets. Even if they do, there isn't much on this planet that could even dent the shuttle. The most they could do is scratch the paint or graffiti it, and even then the local patrols would be notified."

"The patrols have enough to deal with."

"Then we get a cool new paint job." Teal winked and gave Emerson a squeeze.

Dollard skulked down the ramp and Reggie followed. The ship sealed up automatically as they left it behind. They descended the wooden planks acting as stairs into the building. The squad was waiting at the landing on the second floor.

Azikiwe saluted. "All clear, sir."

"At ease." Reggie looked down the ratty hallway. The sour smell of filth and dilapidation wafted over him. He had the brief memory of running down identical hallways as a child, and pushed it aside. "We've got a stop to make. I'm hoping we can take a shortcut to The Neon Heart, but I need some information. Even what I can remember is all out of date by now. Let's keep our heads down, our eyes up, and make as little commotion as possible."

The soldiers nodded. Teal smiled. Dollard looked to the distance, as if interested in the minds of the people around them. Emerson stuck next to Teal, her face still pale.

"I'll take the lead. Hopefully I won't get us too lost, but alert me to anything you think is urgent." Reggie took a shallow breath in the fetid hallway and prepared for the rest of what the Wall had to offer.

"Let's go."

When they reached the ground level, they turned north, towards the top-half of the city. They snaked through tight corridors littered with people at ramshackle booths selling junk, or just laying in the way. Some scurried for shadows and smaller alleyways at the sight of the soldiers, most just took a casual glance and went about their business. Progress was slow with the party—even as small as seven. Reggie led them to a few dead ends, one so narrow that they had to shuffle back in a single file.

Teal caught up to him and looped an arm around his. "Know where we're going, Captain?"

"Sure. Pretty sure. Where's your shadow?" Reggie continued to look forward, checking the surrounding streets against his memory.

"Just behind. She's pretty focused on keeping you blocked. Good kid."

"Thanks for looking out for her." Reggie stopped, peered down an alley to their right, shook his head and kept going forward.

"Meh. Someone had to take her off your hands." Teal scanned the stalls as they passed, absentmindedly checking their wares.

"What's that mean?" Reggie glanced at her.

"Just that you're a protective papa and if someone wasn't watching that poor girl you'd be doting over her, not giving your full attention to the mission."

Reggie shrugged. "I suppose."

Teal poked him in the ribs. "Any words for the troops?"

"Getting restless?"

"Not them. Me."

"I'm pretty confident we're going in the right direction. It's a maze." Reggie wiped his brow. "It's hot, right?"

"Also me." Teal winked and slinked back in line.

Dollard signaled Reggie through the comm-band. "I'm getting something up ahead. Not the crowd."

"I got it too," Hoa added.

Reggie put up his fist to stop the group. "Form-up."

Teal slipped next to him again, her machine pistol drawn as if she had been waiting to use it. The soldiers fanned out in the back, making a squat arrow shape. Dollard and Emerson huddled in the middle of the armed and armored squad members.

As soon as they were in position, the narrow street emptied. People scrambled for doors, alleys, and the mock safety of their wooden stalls. Seemingly boarded up windows flew open and people dressed in bright red with shocks of dyed hair and red dancing tattoos opened fire with old rifles, bolt throwers, and pistols.

The soldiers fired back, each aiming for a window, filling it—and the person occupying it—with flecks of irradiated aluminum from their top-of-the-line shock rifles.

Reggie brought his pistol up and fired, aiming precisely to cause maximum damage with each shot. Teal sprayed wildly, holding her gun out far and up high, turning in place. She screamed over the sound of her machine pistol ripping through ammunition at a furious pace.

Dollard spoke over the comm. "There are more coming. At least two other groups."

"Maybe they'll keep each other busy?" Reggie took flak from a shotgun across his sleeve. His jacket stopped the pellets and rippled with their colour. The spray managed to hit his hand and spread to his neck. He grimaced at the pain and tingling in his arm as he aimed at another target.

"Possibly, but there will certainly be more attention focused on us."

Reggie nodded and patched in with the group. "We're moving."

"Alley to the right," Dollard said.

"You get that?"

"Hup," Azikiwe said, speaking for the squad.

"I think we've got them on the run." Teal let out a whoop and reloaded. The long clip dropped out of her gun and she pulled a replacement from her jacket, slamming it into place.

"That wasn't a suggestion. Let's go." Reggie shuffled for the alley, taking slow steps so the squad could keep the formation and wrangle Dollard and Emerson in the middle.

When they got to the mouth, he stopped, covering their retreat. "Azikiwe. Take the lead. There's a building at the end of the alley. Get inside and make sure it's empty. I'd like to get off the streets to figure this one out."

The soldier didn't answer, but Reggie heard footfalls as she made her way down the alley. He leaned around the corner, keeping an eye on the gang that was attacking them and picking off anyone getting too close. Without consciously thinking about it, his jacket shifted colours, blending in with the brown and beige bricks of the building he hugged.

Teal came on the comm-band. "Making a last stand already?"

"Just working out a little frustration, making sure we're not being followed too closely."

"Need some company?"

He shook his head. "Keep Emerson and Dollard secure. I won't be long."

Behind him, a dozen meters down the alley, a door burst open between him and the squad. Three figures in red and black torn shirts and pants, tattoos and spiked hair rushed out, screaming. One opened his mouth wider than Reggie thought should be possible and yelled, his long, forked tongue flailing around, spraying bloody saliva.

"Shit." Reggie spun to face them, let off a shot, and charged.

The bullet hit the one with the tongue, but the man didn't slow down. As he closed the distance, Reggie slipped under a wild swing. He caught the man's arm, wedging it between his elbow and side as it swiped back. The crazed man screamed in Reggie's face. A smack with the butt end of Reggie's pistol shut him up.

A spray of bullets hit the ground and walls around them. "Watch where you're shooting, Teal!"

"Stay with the group, Reggie!"

Reggie peered around the big body he was struggling with. The two other gang members were charging the squad. Teal kept them busy with bursts from her automatic pistol.

"Okay." Reggie kicked the man he was fighting in the back of the knee, forcing his mass to drop. The grip he had on the man's arm backfired, though, and he was pulled down too. As he tumbled forward, Reggie flipped his pistol to grab the barrel. It was hot from his repeated shots, but before it could burn him, he swung the butt end and hit the freak behind the ear. The man slumped, letting go of Reggie, but he screamed, his mouth opening wider, pulling open tears at the sides. At close range, Reggie pumped several rounds into the man's chest and face until he stopped moving.

Before he could catch his breath, Reggie got to his feet and ran at the other gang members closing on his squad. He chose the closest one and took aim. "I've got mine," he said to Teal over the comm-band.

"Uh-huh."

He saw Teal drop to a knee, causing both men to falter. The two operatives took their shots nearly in unison, dropping their targets. With the path clear, he jogged back to the squad, slipping into position next to Teal.

"They went down easier than that guy with the forked tongue. He must have been on something crazy." Reggie breathed heavily and swallowed.

"I managed to glean the answer for that one," Dollard said. "They are on a street drug called Blender. Seems to be the narcotic of choice in the Wall at the moment. Most of that gang were tweaked out on it, but the gentleman you tangled with had taken quite a dosage."

Reggie cleared his throat. "You're telling me." He nodded to Azikiwe.

The squad moved to a doorway at the end of the alley. Azikiwe kicked her the door open and disappeared inside. A moment later she called for everyone to come through.

Reggie pushed the broken door closed behind him and looked around the space. They were in an abandoned factory. Old rusted machines the size of their shuttle, rested like slumbering beasts evenly spaced across the dusty floor. Faint yellow paint marked safety zones around them. Narrow windows set high on the walls let in dim light through their filthy panes of glass.

Reggie checked his pistol. The charge was nearly full and the copper slug had thousands of shots left.

"Now, any idea why they attacked us?"

Teal kicked a large bolt, sending it bounding across the floor. "Either way, I'm calling in a strike on those assholes. The audacity to attack corporate—"

"No." Reggie picked at the pellets in his hand. "We still have a long way to go. No need to put everyone in the Wall on alert. The lower gangs don't need to know we're coming."

"They already do. At least some of those red freaks are going to spread the news."

"And we don't need to help them." Reggie checked the time on his personal display. It took them over an hour to get to the surface and they'd been there for less than two. "We've got twenty hours to find the Heart and get back."

Hoa stepped forward. "I have a thought."

Reggie nodded.

"I noticed that the gang was waiting for us. It was either just dumb luck that we happened to go in the same direction where they had set up a trap, or they are way more organized than any gang I've dealt with anywhere I've been."

"Or," Reggie said. "They knew we were coming."

"Right," Hoa said.

"Well, let's not jump to conclusions. In this place, anything is possible. We've got a job to do."

"What's the next move?" Azikiwe asked.

"We keep heading north. We're close to one of the exits. I've got to see a man about a shortcut. Then we go down."

"Hup," the soldiers said in unison.

"I still want to call it in," Teal said.

"Save it. We're supposed to be under the radar." Reggie turned to Dollard and Emerson. "How are you two holding up?"

"I'm handling my task just fine." Dollard had his eyes closed, likely searching their surroundings.

"And you?" Reggie glared at Emerson.

She looked up at him. Her eyes seemed sunken, the dark circles around them more pronounced in the dim light. "It's." She nodded. "I'm fine. I can handle it."

"I want you to let me know if it's becoming a strain. I expect there will be all sorts of people wanting to poke around in our heads. If you can stop them, great. If it's difficult, do your best, but tell me."

Emerson nodded and shut her eyes.

Reggie pulled another shotgun pellet from the side of his hand. "Let's get moving. Azikiwe, after you."

NINE

GRAVES

Reggie sent Azikiwe to check a blind alley. They moved slowly through less populated routes, the soldiers clearing buildings before the group crossed through them. Azikiwe peered around the brick wall and darted across the mouth of the alley. She scanned the space again and gave the all clear.

They joined her and they headed down the narrow gap in single file. Teal held Reggie back as the others shuffled forward.

"What are you doing, Reg?"

He furrowed his brow. "What do you mean?"

"This plodding forward is painful. We're not getting anywhere."

"It's better than another ambush. Besides, we're close."

"Close to where?" she sighed.

"There's an information broker, old crackpot,

but he knows something that I'd like to know. He's set up by one of the north entrances and we're nearly there."

"We'd better be, this crawling forward is killing me. And, aren't you on a timeline?"

"That, you don't need to remind me of. Get going."

They crossed through another building that opened to a main thoroughfare and followed it north. Stalls were set up in the spaces between structures, clogging the passage, forcing people to hear what the vendors were yelling.

Reggie spotted a gate leading out of the Wall and urged the group forward. They gathered near the large opening.

"This is it. Everyone keep your eyes peeled. Azikiwe, I don't want you to go far, but check out our options of egress. I want to know the way is clear, depending on what direction we go."

The soldier nodded, made some hand signals to her squad, and they scattered.

Reggie turned to Dollard. "See if you can pick up anything about that red gang we met earlier. If something else spikes your interest, follow the lead, but I want to figure out what that gang knows sooner or later."

Dollard didn't look. "Already on it." He sighed.

"What about me?" Teal asked. "And Emerson?"

She put an arm around the girl, pulling her close.

"Stick with me. We're going to see a man about an elevator."

"Finally." Teal pulled Emerson along behind Reggie.

"It hasn't been that long." Reggie scanned the stalls, looking for an old computer monitor and stacks of paper.

"Two hours." Teal drew out the words, adding a groan at the end.

"Well, we're here now. If this pans out, we'll cut out the majority of this trip."

Reggie spotted the stall he was looking for and walked up to the rotting wooden counter. An old man, thin with bulbous joints, looked up behind broken glasses.

"Graves. Just who I've been looking for."

The old man slunk back behind the counter—his eyes, huge behind the glasses, searched Reggie up and down.

"I have nothing for corporate interests. Nothing of value, nothing you'll have any interest in."

The smell of the old man reached Reggie, making him hesitate, but he leaned forward. "Take a look, you old codger. It's me."

"Me? Me? Who is me? There are thousands of me and one Graves. Don't torment an old man." Graves sunk farther behind his counter.

A guard by the gate chuckled. "Got yourself some corporate trouble, eh Graves? Serves you right."

Reggie waved the woman off. She sneered at him, but left. "Okay, enough games. Even if you don't remember me, I need info and I've got a corporate account to pay for it."

"Pay, yes. Pay you will." Graves shed the timid act and stood. "I have information and you have credits. Clearly you know that I know more about the Wall—"

"Yeah, yeah. I'm in a hurry. I need to get to The Neon Heart."

Graves clicked his tongue and shook his head. "A very dangerous prospect."

"You're telling me. I know there's an elevator. I'm not sure where, and I don't know how to access it, but I'm willing to pay a whole lot of Amcoral's money to skip trudging down there on foot."

Graves held out his hand. "Payment first."

"You've got the info I need?" Reggie side-eyed the old man.

"I do, but you will not like what I have to say."

Reggie glanced at Teal. She was on her tiptoes, grinning madly. "I can't wait to see this."

"How much?"

"One thousand."

"Credits? You're nuts."

"And you are desperate." Graves planted a crooked hand on a stack of filthy paper.

Reggie rubbed his chin. "If I'm not going to like the information, I want a discount."

"That is the discounted price, young man."

Nodding, Reggie tapped on his comm-band, transferring the credits to the old man. "Alright, spill."

"There is an elevator that descends the lower levels and goes right into the Heart. It is close, no more than an hour's walk, depending on conditions of the Wall."

"Go on."

"It is locked. Only guests with the proper chip can access it, and then it can only be controlled by an operator in The Neon Heart."

Teal put her chin on Reggie's shoulder. "We'll see about that."

Reggie shrugged her off. "What else?"

Graves smiled. "Very astute, corporate man. It is under guard. It's under corporate guard."

"Corporate? Not Telbak?"

"No, something else." Graves smiled wider.

"Someone's making a play." Reggie looked down the alley, thinking of what corporation would know and be making a move for the Heart.

"That's stupid," Teal said. "With Amcoral and Telbak making a claim, who would be dumb enough to try and beat them?"

"Especially for something that doesn't exist." Reggie rubbed his chin.

"Oh, it does exist. At least something exists that is causing all this ruckus." Graves coughed. He wiped his hand on his shirt.

"Do you know what company is guarding the elevator?" Reggie asked Graves.

"I can't tell you apart. All false gods lording over the surface, cutting it up as you see fit."

"Right." Reggie rolled his eyes. "What else can you tell me?"

"I can tell you that there is no way to take the elevator down. Even if you make it on board, the one controlling it in The Neon Heart will keep you on the surface."

Teal stepped forward. "Weren't you listening when I said we'll see about that—because we will definitely see about that. I can hack some Earth elevator."

"That is, if we can get past whoever is guarding it," Reggie said. He turned to Graves again. "One last thing. You said we can't take it down. What is the situation once we get inside the bar?"

"Ah. More astute than I gave you credit for. If you can make it to the Heart, if you can get in, and if you find what you are looking for, there should be no trouble making your way back to the surface."

"Lots of ifs," Teal said.

"Let's go see what we're working with, then we can make some decisions." Reggie called the soldiers over the comm-band and spotted Dollard a few meters away. "Can you give me the route to the elevator from here?"

Graves squinted at him. "Perhaps. You know the nature of the Wall, don't you?"

"Give me your best estimate. We'll take it from there."

"Very well." Graves took a scrap of paper and scribbled down a list of instructions. It was hard to read, but Reggie thought he could follow the directions.

"Thanks."

As Reggie took the paper, Graves grabbed his wrist. "Your brother is missed. He was a far better man than you turned out to be. He would not have abandoned us to those false masters."

Reggie pulled free. "You do recognize me. Old nutcase."

With the paper in hand and his group gathered, Reggie led them towards the elevator.

THE NEON HEART

TEN
BLOCKED PATH

Reggie kicked the stone wall. "Another dead end." He turned to see the group in a ragged line behind him. "Let's go back to the junction and hook left. We should be close."

Dollard threw his arms up. "This is a waste of time."

Teal leaned on his shoulder. "Welcome to the Wall."

The soldiers led the way back out of the alley, to a courtyard with overgrown patches of weeds and a cracked fountain dribbling brown water.

Reggie looked at the sheet of paper he'd gotten from Graves, going over their route in his mind. "From what I can make out, it's on the other side of that wall. Let's take the right path here and see if we can go around." He pointed to a broken sidewalk that led to an alley in the shadows of a squat structure with floors added in wood and a huge complex turned to tenements. Signs dotting the exterior advertised the various businesses scattered through, making the building look like it was infected with some kind of pox.

The alley turned sharply at a wall wedged between two structures, joining them together. It followed to a fence blocking the way forward. Reggie looked up at the building on the far side of the fence. The facade was huge, taller than the buildings around it with their extensions reaching half-again, or more, over their roofs. It was more extravagant, too. Designed to impress and impose with rounded corners and dated ornate features.

Reggie gave a signal, and the soldiers silently scurried to the wooden barrier. Muller dropped to a knee and Hoa stepped on his open hands. He lifted her so she could just peek over the top of the fence. A split second later, she dropped and they came back.

"Report," Azikiwe said.

Hoa looked up and away, reviewing what her implant recorded. "There is definitely something there. A squad, two dozen, maybe more around the corner. They are posted in front of a large door. Maybe a garage? The building over there is big. It's a whole complex on its own."

She blinked and nodded at Reggie, sending what

she saw to his lenses. At a prompt he gave access to the rest of the group.

"That's the place." Reggie focused on the recording. "I haven't been to The Neon Heart, but I know it's on the bottom floor of an old complex. At one time it was the headquarters for some corporation back when governments were in charge."

"And this is it?" Azikiwe studied her own view of Hoa's recording.

"It fits, and—" He spotted the black and red uniforms the soldiers were wearing and frowned at Teal. "What the hell is the Consortium doing here?"

Teal put a hand to her face. "Making our lives a lot more difficult."

Azikiwe stepped forward. "Excuse me, Commander. What is the Consortium?"

Reggie sighed. "It's not supposed to be real. It's a group of some of the smaller corporations that apparently made a secret unapproved merger under the nose of the Council. If what I've heard of them is correct, and we can't assume anything anyone has heard is true, combined they rival both Amcoral and Telbak. Because they're made up of a bunch of smaller corporations, they have a ton of holdings, just nothing particularly impressive."

"Which helps them keep under the radar," Teal said.

"We dealt with them on a colony assignment a

few years ago." Reggie pressed his lips together. "They've got to be the ones who sent those red gang people after us."

"Should we call it in?" Azikiwe asked.

Reggie shook his head. "No. We're trying to keep a low profile. It'll stir up a hornets' nest that will go nowhere fast. We've got a time limit, they have deniability. Dollard?"

"I'm on it." The Esper walked to the fence and put his hand out. "They definitely have a reader with them. I'll try to—" Turning, he stared wide eyed at Reggie. "They made us."

The soldiers got between the fence and the rest of the group, weapons up. Dollard ran past them to the middle of the formation. Reggie and Teal pulled their own weapons.

"Back, slowly," Reggie said.

Emerson tugged on his sleeve. "I can stop them. I can make the Esper think he didn't sense anything."

"You can do that?" Reggie raised an eyebrow.

"I can if I stop protecting you. Just for a minute. I can block them." The girl clenched her teeth, struggling against something.

"Do it." Reggie put up a hand to stop Azikiwe. "Hold here, be ready."

Dollard put his fingers to his temples. "I've got five approaching, one is the Esper."

Emerson closed her eyes and seemed to flex her

whole body. She shook, her hands in tight fists.

"They've stopped," Dollard whispered.

Everyone held their breath and watched Emerson. Reggie caught Azikiwe's eyes and the soldier flinched. He gestured towards the fence with a nod and she spun, covering the direction with her rifle again. The other two soldiers did the same.

Reggie looked at Teal and she shrugged. He frowned and tried to decide between holding fast and retreating before it was too late.

"They're moving away," Dollard said. "The Esper is—not—looking for us anymore."

Teal let out a long sigh.

Emerson stayed tensed, focused. Reggie put a hand on her shoulder and the girl jumped.

"You did it. Good job."

She was sweating and looked even more pale. She swayed on her feet and Reggie caught her.

"Whoa, it's okay. Power down." He held her up.

"You—you're not—" Her head rolled back.

Reggie lowered her to a sitting position and leaned her against a wall. He opened one of her eyes and checked her vision. Her pupils contracted and he relaxed. He put his hand on her forehead, feeling heat radiating from the girl.

"Don't worry. We're good right now. Just relax. Focus on breathing."

Teal squatted down beside them. "That really

kicked your ass, eh kid?"

"Maybe it wasn't such a good idea," Reggie said.

"I'm okay." Emerson struggled to sit up.

Reggie pushed her back. "There's no rush. They don't seem to know we're here."

Teal took out a canteen and helped the girl take a sip. She nudged Reggie.

He nodded and stood. "Dollard. How's it looking?"

"They are in the same position as when we arrived. Some are just standing by the door, four seem to be on a patrol route."

"I assume there is an elevator behind that door?"

"Yes. It's the cause of a lot of trepidation in the group."

Reggie squinted. "They're scared?"

"Of the things in the lower levels. Of a Corporate raid."

"Keep an eye on them."

Dollard nodded and closed his eyes.

Reggie joined the soldiers. "From the look of things, the elevator is a no go. Any options?"

Azikiwe shrugged. "You're the commander."

"Yeah." Reggie looked towards the fence. "Alright. If they've got it locked up, there is no way we're taking the quick way down. Time to cut our losses. We head to the nearest stairwell and start our descent."

Azikiwe nodded. She made some gestures with her hand, sending her two troopers out wide, covering the group. She stayed in the middle, watching the fence.

Teal had Emerson back on her feet. Reggie went over. "We're taking the scenic route."

"Right. I think we're ready to go." Teal rubbed Emerson's back.

The girl nodded. "I'm good. You're covered."

"Don't push yourself like that again. If you need to drop my coverage, do it." Sighing, Reggie waved the rest of the group over. "We passed a stairwell back in that courtyard. It's as good a place as any."

THE NEON HEART

ELEVEN

DOWN

Reggie stood at the top of the stairs. The light pouring around him from the surface didn't reach the first landing. Cool air wafted up, bringing with it smells of earth, filth, and rot. Azikiwe stood next to him. She shone the light from her rifle down the stairwell. The bright white beam forced the shadows into the corners, showing trash collected in a pile at the first turn.

"This isn't going to be fun, but keep the formation we've used so far. Watch every corner, go slowly," Reggie said.

Azikiwe nodded and called her troops over. They descended with her taking the lead, the other two a step behind. Dollard and Emerson followed, the expert Esper holding his nose.

Teal grabbed Reggie's arm, stopping him. "You ready for this, champ?"

"Don't have much of a choice. Time's ticking away too quickly, we have a long way to go."

"Follow your own advice. Don't push yourself too hard. Last time you were here—"

"That was a long time ago. But, thanks." Reggie gestured to the stairwell, and Teal descended. He followed, pistol out. His lenses adjusted to the darkness automatically.

The stairs wound down three flights before reaching the first subterranean floor. L1 was spray-painted on the wall along with several gang tags marked on top of each other. Reggie noticed the distinct image of a face sprayed in red with a forked tongue. He grimaced, but didn't mention it to the rest of the group.

Light fixtures set high along the hallway shone dim yellow light that made Reggie squint. They buzzed loudly and several flickered in conflicting patterns. Concentrating, he made his contact lenses adjust the colour to tint to light blue, making it easier to see and less harsh on his eyes. He saw Teal whispering to Emerson, presumably telling the girl to do the same with her implant.

Azikiwe led the soldiers forward. They stopped at every door and open doorway—one darting across, the other two providing cover. It was slow moving, but they sped up as they went.

Dollard had one hand up, the other to his temple. He swiped back and forth like a radar dish, checking the rooms. Reggie caught up with him.

"Anything?"

Dollard sighed. "Not if you're going to hover over me like a nanny."

Reggie forced a smile. "Right. Keep me posted."

They moved to the end of the hallway where the wall was smashed open and a rough tunnel connected to the next building. Reggie signaled for the soldiers to keep going. The lights in the adjoining building were brighter allowing them to see the stains on the carpet. It squished as they walked across it, a mystery of mixed fluids pooling around their steps. They reached another stairwell at the end of the hall and continued to descend to the bottom. Reggie saw a smaller L4 painted on the wall, along with the graffiti that covered most of the walls.

Azikiwe stopped him. "Any idea how many levels we're going?"

"I've never reached the bottom, but it's somewhere around fifty."

The soldier's eyes widened. "Fifty?"

"Most of the Wall doesn't reach that far, but that's the lowest I know of. It's mostly additions that far down, basically caves except for the few old buildings large enough to have subbasements. The Neon Heart should be somewhere around those original lowest levels, but no one knows how far it really goes."

"How do we find it?"

"We keep going down. Eventually we'll be in the right area."

Azikiwe's shoulders dropped. "That could take days. And the lower we go, the more dangerous it will be."

"Yeah. It's a pickle all right. Good thing I know the coordinates of the building with the lowest floor."

"The elevator."

Reggie nodded. "It's not going to make the trip any easier, but it should save some wandering." He checked the time on his display. "Just about eighteen hours left. Let's keep moving."

The soldier straightened. "Yes, sir." She moved, her troops joining in the sweep.

The group made it halfway down the hallway and a door opened. The soldiers pointed their weapons and Dollard and Emerson slipped behind Teal and Reggie.

"Stop there," Azikiwe said.

An old woman in a filthy housecoat screamed and dropped a bag of trash. She slammed her door.

"Damn." Reggie waved the soldiers ahead. They lowered their weapons. "Double time."

"It was just an old woman," Dollard said.

Teal tucked her machine pistol into its holster.

"Underground, any commotion is going to get to the nearest gang. It may seem like a quiet, disgusting tenant building, but anything could be behind these doors."

"Let's go before she tells someone we're here," Reggie said.

The group jogged to the end of the hall. It turned left and met a junction. They went left again and reached another stairwell. Reggie heard doors opening behind them.

"Hurry." They clamored down in a loose formation, Reggie staying at the back. Before he followed the group, he spotted several figures gathering near the intersection. He squatted on the stairs so he was just peeking over the top. He noticed his sleeve as his coat blended in with the stained grey carpet. Focusing, he made the lenses zoom in on the group. There were half a dozen people he could see, and they were all wearing prominent red clothing with the same dancing red tattoos as the gang that had ambushed them. He connected to the others over the comm, giving them a view of what he saw.

"We're going to have some company and they probably know all about us already."

"Who the hell are these people?" Teal asked.

Dollard made a humming sound. "They call themselves... The... The Red Gang."

"Not very creative," Teal said.

"They don't have to be, there are a lot of them, especially around here. The word is going out," Dollard added.

"Great." Reggie backed away and bounded down the stairs to catch up with the group. "What's the stairwell look like?"

"It continues for several levels," Azikiwe said.

"Keep going. I'm right behind you." Using the railing to swing himself around corners, Reggie skipped steps, trying to make it to the others. He heard the sound of the Red Gang members reaching the stairwell, chasing after him.

He got to the next floor and shots came at him from the hallway. Diving to the side, he avoided the first barrage. He rolled and tumbled down the next set of stairs, hitting the landing in a heap. Pulling himself to his feet, he drew his pistol. A few shots hit the wall above him and he darted for the next set of steps.

"They've got friends and they are right on my heels." Reggie huffed as he descended as quickly as he could.

"We have met some of them farther down. Do you need assistance?" Azikiwe asked.

Reggie heard weapons fire over the comm. "I'm not far. Keep going until you hit a dead end and find a place to make a stand if you have to. I'll be bringing more guests to the party."

At the next floor, Reggie hesitated, causing the waiting ambush to fire ahead of him. He jumped the last few steps, landing into a roll. Firing blindly, he dashed to the stairs. He heard more shots coming from farther below and jumped the rest of the way, crashing into the wall as he landed. Grabbing a bottle from the trash gathered in the corner, he glanced down the stairs. He spotted a large L7 scrawled on the wall a level below him and prepared for more people shooting at him.

Tossing the bottle, the waiting gang members fired, giving him another window. With a jump, he swung himself round the railing. A shot hit him in the back, impacting his jacket and shoving him forward. The air was pushed out of his lungs and he stumbled. Catching the railing, he stopped his fall and heaved in ragged breaths. He forced himself to crawl down the stairs and spotted his squad at the level eight landing.

The soldiers were pressed against the walls, exchanging fire with gang members in the corridor. A discarded dresser was tipped on its side, providing minimal cover. Teal was on her belly, spraying her machine pistol wildly. Dollard and Emerson were hiding on the stairs and flinched as Reggie approached them.

He coughed, trying to speak. He calmed himself and caught his breath.

"More on the way. Get ready."

TWELVE
FIREFIGHT

Teal rolled onto her back and looked up at Reggie. "We're stuck here!"

"It's either forward or back and there are a whole lot of them on their way."

Stomping footsteps cascaded down the stairwell. Reggie leaned around the railing, his pistol out.

Azikiwe called over the comms. "There are half a dozen of them in this hallway. They have better positioning than we do, but we have better weapons. It's a stalemate."

"Then we have to do something to shake things up." Reggie saw the first gang member clattering down the stairwell and shot him. The man, with a thick, bright red beard and dressed in a ripped red t-shirt, fell back, dead. The people behind him stopped.

Reggie took the moment yell to Dollard. "Anything you can glean to get us out of this?"

"I can tell you they want us dead and think we're doomed. Does that help?"

"Not really." A head peeked around the corner and Reggie drove it back with another shot.

"I have an idea, but it's stupid," Teal said over the comm.

Reggie let off another shot to make the next person in line rethink coming any farther. "It's better than sitting here until we're overrun."

"Not much."

"You going to tell me?"

"Yeah, but you aren't going to like it."

"Spit it out, Teal." Reggie leaned back and shifted his footing.

"That new jacket of yours is bulletproof, right?"

"It's puncture proof, doesn't do anything against the impact."

"Better than me. We swap positions and you run out, making those folks aim at you."

"I already hate it. Go on."

"That should get them out of position so the others can get an angle on them."

Reggie leaned around the other side of the stairwell to meet Teal's eyes. "You know the rest of me is exposed, right?"

She shrugged. A slug hit the dresser next to her, sprinkling her with splintered wood.

"Okay, quick swap."

Rolling back on her stomach, Teal scrambled up the stairs on all fours. Reggie hopped over her and slid into position behind the dresser next to Muller. The soldier nodded at him and popped up to shoot over the top of the makeshift cover.

Reggie snuck a glance, pulling back just before a bullet hit where his head had been. A couch was set up lengthwise as a barrier, nearly covering wall to wall. Farther down, open doors and more furniture acted as cover for the gang.

"If I cause a distraction, can you guys take these shitheads out before they kill me?"

Azikiwe nodded. "Absolutely."

Muller shook his head.

Hoa shrugged.

Reggie huffed. "Oh, crap. Okay. You ready?" His jacket shifted to match the colour of the dresser and the carpet as he zipped it up.

The soldiers let out their 'hup' reply.

Pistol in hand, Reggie rocked in place, getting ready to charge the gang members who had them pinned at the bottom of the stairs.

"Now!" Rolling out from behind the dresser, Reggie shot blindly as he got to his feet. He ran to the couch, sliding as he approached. Bullets, slugs, and buckshot filled the space above him. He hit the front of the couch hard, and rolled onto his back. A woman in a fitted red jacket covered in spikes came over the top, the shotgun in her hand searching for him. Her head was jerked back by a round from the soldiers, and her limp body fell onto him. Pushing her off, he gave a thumbs up. The soldiers seemed to aim and fired rapidly, changing targets as the enemy dropped.

Reggie watched them duck back behind the dresser as the remaining gang members retaliated.

"We got most of them, but some are staying hidden," Azikiwe said over her implant.

Reggie looked at the couch. It was overstuffed and had thick wooden armrests. The fabric was a garish flower pattern, but faded and covered in layers of stains and grime. He put his foot against it and pushed. It was heavy but slid on the short hallway carpet.

"I have an idea. Be ready." Getting to his knees, making sure to stay in cover, he put his shoulder into the ratty front of the couch. He heard a spray of bullets coming from up the stairwell and clenched his teeth. "Go."

He grunted as he pushed. He struggled as it hit the first obstruction, likely a dead body, but momentum kept it moving. The impact from the gang shooting at him reverberated through the wood and fabric. The sound of the soldiers returning fire pierced through the noise.

The back of the couch slammed into the first open doors, closing them, stopping Reggie. He'd made about three metres.

Huffing, he dropped to the floor and looked back at the stairwell. Azikiwe jumped over the dresser and sprinted down the hall. She slipped next to him. Muller and Hoa ran up the stairs to join Teal.

"That's nearly all of them. Big push from behind," Azikiwe said.

"What's left?"

"Two, one behind a door, the other behind a stove."

"You want left or right?" Reggie glanced over the top of the couch and spotted the stove sitting along the right wall.

"I'll take the door."

Reggie nodded. "Your count."

Azikiwe counted to three and they hopped the couch. The soldier leveled her rifle at the door and blew a hole the size of a melon through it—and the man on the other side. Reggie ran for the stove. The woman using it for cover, her hair a bright red tangled nest, stood and aimed at him. He brought his foot up and kicked the stove, toppling it onto her. Letting out a groan, the woman raised her weapon, and he shot her.

Turning back to the stairs, Reggie yelled for the others. "Let's go!" He tapped Azikiwe on the arm.

"Have Muller and Hoa watch our backs, you and I will take the lead."

Nodding, Azikiwe gave the orders though her implant. "They're on it."

"Eyes open." Reggie jogged to the end of the hallway, his group following in a staggered line. He heard the odd gunshot from the gang chasing them, or the soldiers covering their retreat. The corridor opened to the left, and he followed it, eyeing doorways and the odd discarded items large enough for someone to hide behind. He reached the next turn to the left, but a tunnel was dug into the wall, continuing forward. Reggie stopped and ran through their progress so far, his hands waving with the turns he remembered.

"Straight is west, right?" He looked back at Azikiwe.

The soldier was covering down the left hallway. She looked up, accessing her implant. "Yeah."

"This way." Reggie picked up their pace, running through the tunnel. The ground was wet and squished where he stepped. He saw footprints among the other filth on the carpeted hallway floor. "Shit."

Teal caught up with him, Emerson and Dollard stuck to her like remoras attached to a larger fish. "What's the holdup? They're right behind us."

Reggie pointed to the footsteps. "It won't be

hard for them to follow."

"Nothing we can do about that now." Teal ran past him.

The paint in the new hallway was smudged, dingy, and flaking off. Many of the overhead lights were smashed, bits of glass and wire scattered under the fixtures.

Reggie followed Teal, Emerson and Dollard now stuck to him. He turned to the Esper. "I don't suppose you—"

"Too many people, too much divergence. That red gang on our tail is overwhelming everything." Dollard huffed. Beads of sweat at his brow ran down his face, dragging the makeup with it.

"Okay." He turned to Emerson and met her eyes. He raised an eyebrow. "You good?"

She pursed her lips and nodded. "It's hot."

"Yeah. It is getting warmer. Keep the jacket on until we're clear." Reggie waited for her to pass and unzipped his own jacket.

Teal was at the end of the hall, waiting for them. Reggie heard her over his comm-band.

"More stairs going down. Looks like they go a long way."

"That'd be nice if we didn't have a bunch of thugs and delinquents on our heels." Reggie stopped. "Form up there. I'll bring them to you."

Dollard and Emerson slowed, looking back at

Reggie. He waved them towards Teal and went back to the tunnel.

Azikiwe was still there, crouched with her rifle ready.

"Where are Hoa and Muller?"

"On their way. They're staggering, covering each other. Takes time."

Reggie rubbed his chin. "Stay here. Keep watching the tunnel. I'll see if I can help them out."

Running back to the turn, Reggie checked the charge on his pistol. He edged to the corner, putting his back to the wall. Risking a glance, he spotted Muller duck into an open doorway as Hoa fired at the red gang from behind the couch.

He called their comms. "I'm here. Right side. I'll cover you."

"Got it," Muller said.

"Yup." Hoa kept firing.

Several of the red gang goons were clustered on the stairwell. Some hid behind the dresser, but the rifles the soldiers used tore through the wood, leaving it full of holes and partially collapsed. The remaining gang members used the bodies of their fallen friends as cover. Reggie picked off one, then another, keeping them back on the landing. Hoa took the opening to run to the cover Muller left, the older soldier already running to Reggie's position. When Muller reached the corner, he slipped in under

Reggie in a crouch and joined in on the suppressing fire. Hoa darted from the doorway taking a slug in the shoulder. She stumbled, but kept crawling towards them.

Muller sprang from cover, firing at the stairwell as he made for his partner. Reggie took aim at the man who had hit Hoa and shot him in the head. The skinny man with a shaved head and red tattoos covering his face collapsed backwards, but someone else took his place.

Dragging Hoa around the corner, Muller dropped his weapon and checked her armor.

"How is she?" Reggie kept his focus on the red gang, holding them on the stairs with consecutive shots.

Hoa grunted as Muller helped her pull her shoulder plate free. "She is fine," Hoa said. "The suit stopped it, but the slug burned through."

"Surface tissue damage, nothing too deep." Muller pulled a canister the size of his thumb from his suit and sprayed the wound.

"Easy for you to say." The goop coated the burn and Hoa sighed. "I'm good. Let's go."

The soldiers stood. "Orders?" Muller asked.

Reggie pulled back from the corner. "Let's give them a reason to hesitate before we go."

Hoa winked at Muller and they changed the settings of their rifles. "We've got something for them."

Reggie grimaced for a moment then shrugged, moving out of the way. The soldiers took positions at the corner.

"Now," Hoa said. She and Muller leaned around the wall and fired. A burst from their rifles pushed both of them back. They went with the momentum, and spun away from the hall.

A series of pops were followed by a blast. A wave of heat rolled down the hallway making Reggie cover his face.

"What the hell was that?"

Hoa stood, smiling. "Micro-nova. Small boom, massive heat. Should incinerate anyone on the stairs and push the rest back. Minimal damage to the structure."

"Huh." Reggie let his mouth hang open.

"See how they like getting burned." Hoa and Muller banged their forearms together, their armor making a dull thud.

"Well, let's go while we can." Reggie gestured for the soldiers to move and they ran towards the rest of the group.

THIRTEEN
THE
SWAMPLAND

Reggie kept track of the levels as the group descended the long stairwell. He put Teal in the lead with Azikiwe and kept himself at the back to cover their escape. The micro-nova Hoa and Muller let off cooked the hallway and the Red Gang seemed to have been stopped there.

The stairwell ended at floor nineteen, by Reggie's count. He called Teal to stop. The atmosphere of the Wall changed as they reached deeper into the underground maze. Brown streaks of liquid trickled down the walls and along cracks, making the air damp. Mold and slime grew in patches and strips. Fewer lights worked, some hallways were completely black, and from the darkness they heard clicks, growls, and other less obvious sounds. More of the structure was made up of makeshift tunnels connecting buildings. Some covered in wood planks or random crap, most bare earth.

Drips collected into acrid puddles on the floor and visible fumes emanated from fungus that grew on the damp ground. The mushroom tops gave off a sheen when light passed over them and held onto the light, faintly glowing from inside.

The group stood in the light cast from the stairwell. Reggie made his way to Teal and checked the time. He had sixteen hours before the ship left him behind.

"It's been quiet." Reggie looked down the hallway. Most of the doors were missing, or broken into piles pushed against the walls.

"Wondering why the Red Gang isn't still following us?" Teal scratched her head and shook out her hair.

"I'm wondering why we haven't run into any other gangs. If the Reds work the surface, they don't control this far down. The nova thing would have pushed them back, but probably would have made them ravenous. Something else stopped them, and not knowing what, bothers me."

Something pale and hunched darted from a doorway and scurried into the shadows.

Teal turned away from the hall and put a hand over her mouth. "Was that a person?"

"Scavenger. I'm surprised it's up this high." Reggie scowled.

"But?"

"Yeah, it's human."

Teal shuttered. "Is it dangerous?"

"Not normally. They get territorial, and it's bad news if you run into a group of them. Mostly they just run away."

"There aren't a lot of people down here. The surface is so packed."

Reggie kept looking where the Scavenger had gone. "There are clusters, but it's not nearly as safe. Most people here have run away from something, or were forced underground."

The sound of Dollard and Hoa arguing drew his attention back to the group.

"Whoa. Keep it down."

The Esper and the soldier were face to face, Emerson struggling to hold Dollard back, the other soldiers holding Hoa. Reggie stepped between them.

"What the hell is going on?"

Dollard sneered and turned away. He went up a few steps.

Hoa shook Azikiwe and Muller off of her and looked away. "Difference of opinion, sir."

"Well, yelling about it when we've just escaped a group of people trying to kill us isn't the best way of handling it." Reggie leaned to get in front of Hoa. "Is it?"

"No, sir."

"Dollard?" Reggie said over his shoulder.

"No."

Reggie rubbed his chin. "Okay. What's going on?"

"We're getting a reading on… something," Hoa said.

"Something?"

Dollard sat on the stairs. "It's hard to make out, but I think it's a group of people."

"It can't be a group, they are all thinking the same thing." Hoa gritted her teeth.

"Don't worry about what you can't agree on. What do you know?"

Hoa sighed. "It's not too close. Down the hallway. Mixed emotions."

"Not mixed, several. Different. Hence multiple people," Dollard said.

"Or conflicted."

Dollard rolled his eyes. "Either way, there are some bad vibes coming from there. I think it's a trap."

Hoa snickered. "Oh, it's definitely a trap."

"The Scavenger," said Teal.

"Yeah." Reggie nodded. "That takes care of this hallway. I wasn't feeling so great about it anyway." He turned back to the group. "Let's try a floor up."

Something in the dark end of the hallway made a noise—a mix of a low growl and a screech. Almost like metal being rent to pieces if it were happening far, far away.

"Better hurry." Reggie nudged Teal towards the stairs and waved at Dollard to get up. He climbed the steps behind them, urging them to go faster.

At the eighteenth floor they stopped to wait for him. The hallway was as damp as the previous one, but more lights worked. On the right wall were doors set farther apart than they had seen. A set of wrist-sized pipes ran down the left wall. They let out a hiss and a sharp spray of mist that made the group jump.

Azikiwe lowered her rifle and adjusted her flak jacket. "Looks different. Almost industrial."

Teal flicked a pipe with a fingernail. The reverberation traveled away from them. "Yeah. Like a basement. Those are probably mechanical rooms, storage. Or they were at some time."

Reggie took a peek down the stairs before joining the group. "This looks better to me." He checked their direction on his comm-band and a compass showed up on his lenses. "This way—unless there is something to worry about down there?"

Dollard put his hand out, as if he was feeling down the hallway. Hoa shrugged.

"It's difficult to say." Dollard shook his head. "It's the same direction as what we were sensing on the floor below. I could be picking up that. Also, there is a general feeling I have been getting since we arrived at the Wall. It's gotten stronger in the lower levels. We are not welcome. Whether that is a hostile feeling or not is difficult to discern. It's omni-present. Each individual I sense has a variation on the theme."

Reggie rubbed his brow. "So, it's probably safe, but no one here likes us. Good enough for me. Azikiwe."

The soldier stood at attention. "Yes, sir."

"Lead the formation. I'll take the back with Teal. Keep heading in the direction of the elevator and keep it tight. I don't like how quiet it's been."

"Hup." Azikiwe nodded to Muller and Hoa and they formed a wedge at the front of the group. Reggie stuck at the back keeping an eye on the stairwell. Teal stayed with him and waited for Dollard and Emerson to get just out of earshot.

"They're getting tired," she said.

Reggie sighed. "Yeah. Still got a long way to go. We'll have to push a little longer."

Teal hugged herself and looked at her feet. "I'm getting tired too. How long are we thinking?"

"It's going to get harder from here. More unpredictable."

"Exactly. We should be facing that fresh."

Reggie frowned. "We can't afford to waste time on multiple rest stops. We're only going to get one if—" He looked away.

"If you're going to make your departure. I get it, Reg. I really do." Teal put a hand on his chest. "These people are all under the gun because of you, but the situation was orchestrated by the Director. It's a mixed bag of shit and I get that you don't like making this more dangerous than it has to be, but you are responsible here. You have to make the hard choice."

"Yeah." Reggie met her gaze. "I'm keeping an eye on the clock, on our progress. I'll make the call before it gets too bad. One reasonable rest rather than a few meager stops."

"Okay."

"Do me a favour?" Reggie looked over Teal's shoulder to the rest of the group. They had passed the first two doors, the soldiers checking for dangers at each one.

"Sure."

"I can manage the soldiers, even Dollard. Watch Emerson for me. I have no idea how hard to push her. I'm worried she'll run herself into the ground."

Teal nodded. "Yeah. She's got something to prove. Reminds me of—"

"—don't." Reggie fought a smile. "I'm not looking to bond with anyone here."

"Oh. I can see a smile." Teal waved her finger in a tiny circle, pointing at his mouth.

Reggie pushed the finger away. "Come on."

THE NEON HEART

FOURTEEN
BARRICADE

The hallway on the eighteenth floor looped around to the left and ended at a cinderblock wall. Reggie clenched his jaw to stop himself from swearing.

"Okay. We knew this would be a maze. Back to the stairwell and we try the next floor up."

Azikiwe swiped at the air with her hand and started walking back the way they'd come. Muller and Hoa fell in a step behind her, creating the wedge, and the others followed. Emerson stopped and Teal walked into her, almost knocking the girl over. Dropping to her knees, Emerson held on to Teal's jacket with one hand and covered her eyes with the other.

"Something is trying to…" Gritting her teeth, Emerson let go of Teal and slumped to the floor.

"Form up!" Reggie drew his pistol and waved Dollard over. "What've you got?"

Eyes wide, Dollard shook his head. "I don't

know. I can't sense anything clearly."

"Wait," Teal said. "You can't sense anything out of the ordinary, or you can't sense anything?"

"Anything, but that kid messes with my readings."

"Emerson?" Teal crouched and rubbed the girl's back. "I need to ask you. Are you blocking Dollard?"

Emerson shook her head sharply, letting out a grunt of effort.

Reggie gave Dollard a shove. "Move, everyone. Azikiwe, double time." He crouched next to Teal. "You got her?"

"Yeah." Teal tried to help Emerson up, but the girl went limp. "Nope."

"Right. Cover our back, I've got her." Scooping up Emerson in his arms, he nodded to Azikiwe. "Go."

With the soldiers in the lead, they jogged to the end of the hall and around the corner towards the stairwell. Reggie adjusted his hold on the limp Emerson to keep her head from rolling back and bumped into Muller.

"Why'd you stop?" He looked up at the tall man.

"Barricade," Muller said.

Reggie leaned around him and saw that the hallway had been blocked almost to the ceiling by a pile of concrete, steel, and stone. "Oh, shit." He heard the sound of people behind the barrier and lowered

Emerson to the floor.

He waved everyone into a huddle. "Options?"

Teal sneered. "Yeah, kick their asses."

"I'm being serious," Reggie said.

"So am I."

Dollard cleared his throat. "I am having trouble getting a clear sense of them. They must have some sort of blocker like that girl." He glanced down at Emerson. "I can tell there are more of them than there are of us."

"It's a bad situation, sir," Azikiwe said. "We're willing to fight it out if you are."

"I don't want to get too hasty. Send someone to check the rooms we've passed—quietly. I'll try to buy us some time." Reggie stood and faced the barricade. He put his hand on a twisted metal girder. At the edge of his vision, he saw Hoa dash back around the corner.

Taking a deep breath, he called out to the people on the other side of the barrier. "Hello? Is there someone I can speak with?"

He heard muffled muttering, but no one answered.

"I want to talk to whoever is in charge."

No one answered and Reggie turned to shrug to the others.

Teal made a fist. "Stop pussyfooting around and give them some hell," she whispered.

Reggie grimaced at her, his hands out in silent exasperation. He looked at Azikiwe and nodded back to the corner. The soldier nodded, checked down the hallway where Hoa went, and shook her head.

Going back to the wall, Reggie rubbed his chin. "Okay. We are not getting anywhere with pleasantries." Teal gave him a thumbs up and Reggie waved her away. "I demand to speak with someone. If not, we will be forced to take action to remove us from this situation." He nodded at the wall.

Teal put a hand on his shoulder. "Good try, tough guy."

Hoa came back around the corner, breathing heavily. "No go. All the rooms are empty and there is no other way out."

"Who is in charge over there? Why have you trapped us?" Reggie yelled.

There were more murmurs on the other side of the barricade but a voice of a woman cut through them. "By now you can see that there is no way out. You are our prisoners. Place your weapons on the ground and line up facing the wall." The words came strongly and steadily. Reggie felt the need to do as he was told. He clenched his fists and pushed the voice out of his head.

The feeling passed, but he was tired, short of breath. He saw the others struggling. Dollard was on his knees, clutching his head and Hoa wavered on her feet. Reggie thought Espers must be more susceptible to whatever she was doing.

Teal was sneering at the barricade, her automatic pistol in hand. "What the hell was that? She's in our heads."

"Must be why Emerson went down. This is bad news."

The woman spoke again. "Do as you are told. You have no chance to escape. There is nowhere for you to go and we have you outnumbered by a vast margin. You may have fancy weapons, but our numbers will overwhelm you." The words hit like a wave against a beach, pushing at their minds, threatening to pull them back out with it. "Now, put your weapons down and stand facing the wall." The tone of her last statement was deeper, adding to her influence.

Reggie fought his hand as it put his pistol on the floor, next to Emerson. Gritting his teeth and clenching as many muscles across his body as he could, he forced himself to stay where he was. With a strain of effort, he turned his head and saw the soldiers walking towards the wall, their rifles on the ground.

Dollard had collapsed and was unconscious. Teal had her gun in hand and was staring at it, her arm shaking as she fought the voice in their heads, commanding their actions.

She looked at Reggie, her face scrunched. "Don't," she managed to squeak. "Don't leave me."

A sharp pain shot through Reggie's head and his legs gave out from under him. He managed to lean away from Emerson and fall backwards. His head bounced off of the floor, making his eyes roll back. He tried to get to his side and push himself up. But he couldn't move his arms.

He tasted blood in his mouth and spat. Fatigue washed over him, making his eyelids heavy. With effort, he turned his head to face Teal. She was still struggling against the command, her free arm fighting the one trying to put her gun on the ground. She frowned through the strain.

Reggie saw the streaks of tears across her cheeks before his vision went black.

FIFTEEN
CAPTURED

Reggie heard grinding then the footsteps of a few dozen people surround the group. He thought he heard a croak from Teal over the noise, but he couldn't focus. Hands grabbed his arms and around his torso, lifting him to his feet. Someone supported him under each arm, keeping him from dropping back down. With a grunt of effort, he managed to lift his head, but his eyes felt glued shut. No one spoke, but Reggie picked out others being lifted and dragged along with him.

He tried counting them, accounting for his crew and had to stop, confused. The order wouldn't come. He'd manage up to three and it would get muddled, so he would try again.

Everything was happening in a daze, like he was being dragged through water. At first, he could tell when they were going down stairs or along a hallway.

He could feel the sensation of his feet dragging over different materials, carpet, wood, dirt, linoleum. Eventually, he could force his eyes open for brief blinks. As the fog lifted and he could keep his eyes open longer, he caught glimpses of the underground complex as they were led through it. He began to step along with the people carrying him, eventually shuffling under his own power. His footsteps clanged against metal grating and he felt a slight rocking back and forth as he walked, but couldn't tell if it was the floor swaying or him.

Reggie thought back to their capture, furrowing his brow. The memories were muddled. He couldn't tell how long it had been or how far they had been taken. Several people were walking in front of him, small and hunched, wearing multiple layers of ragged, filthy clothing. He couldn't make out their shapes under the mass of fabric.

Leaning backwards, he managed to see Teal being carried by four more figures. She struggled in their grip, but she seemed to be tied up. She met Reggie's gaze and fought harder, causing one of the shapes holding her legs to lose its grip. Before she could squirm free, her captor grabbed her feet. She let out a muffled scream and Reggie saw that she was gagged. He thought that she must have put up one hell of a fight.

He tried to pull his arms free of the people holding him, but couldn't get his limbs to follow his instructions. Opening his mouth, he managed a croak, but fell into a coughing fit.

A warm breeze wafted down the hallway towards them and Reggie focused on where he was being carried. At the end of the narrow concrete corridor, he saw a doorway with light pouring in from the room beyond. He blinked, forcing himself to focus on their surroundings. The hallway they were in was just wide enough for him to be flanked on either side by the small people keeping him up and moving. The ceiling was curved and Reggie would have had to duck under it if he wasn't slumped forward. The concrete was stained from leaking water, but the floor was made of metal grating, letting any liquid pool in the space underneath. The metal was solid, but he could see the rust coating everything and places where it was eaten right through.

The doorway they were moving towards was just the hall, or tunnel as it more closely resembled, coming to an end. Squinting, Reggie tried to make out the space, but the light was too bright.

He turned away from it as he was brought through the entrance. The floor changed to a solid stone and through the haze he saw the walls expand outward and the ceiling disappear overhead. As his eyes adjusted, he realized the room wasn't very bright—the hallway they had come from was nearly pitch black. Along the wide, curved walls were more doorways spaced out regularly. In between the open spaces, bunks were bolted to the walls four high and other freestanding stacks of beds haphazardly placed in the middle of the dome-like room. Clusters of figures covered in mounds of clothing sat on the metal bunks, or in groups on the floor. Piles of cases, boxes, crates, and stacked shelves filled with junk made the huge room feel more claustrophobic than the narrow hallway.

Reggie couldn't make out much through the doorways as they passed. Some were small concrete rooms filled with more scavenged stuff. In the middle, on either side, were hallways like the one they had come through. He could see more people clustered among piles of things resembling refuse, but likely thought of as treasured possessions by hoarders. Across the room, where he was being taken, was a third hallway, but this one was wider with regularly spaced out doorways.

A toad hopped onto Reggie's foot. He flinched and it flopped to the floor. Unperturbed, the creature lazily hopped away to join a mass of them gathering around a strange obelisk in one of the rooms. Before Reggie could make out the shapes carved into the pillar, he was shoved into a doorway.

The room was bare concrete, like the rest of the

chamber. The figures carrying Reggie gave him a shove. He stumbled and fell, the control the strange Esper had put him under clung in wisps to his consciousness. Teal kicked as she was placed on the ground, causing one of her captors to drop her. The other squad members, still unconscious, were dumped into a pile like limp sacks of potatoes. The hunched figures hobbled out of the room and slammed shut a heavy metal door with a screech. It didn't sit right in the frame, leaving cracks of light streaming through in odd wedges, but it was large enough to keep them locked inside.

Reggie crawled over to Teal. She was straining against the ropes tying her up. A patch of light showed bruises on her face and a bit of dried blood on her cheek.

"Relax." Reggie's voice was craggy, like he'd been in a deep sleep after a long night of drinking and shouting. He coughed. "Let me work on the knots."

Teal screamed, the rope in her mouth muffling the sound.

Reggie pulled it away and touched her cheek. "Hey. I know. Let me help you and we can figure this out."

She nodded and rolled onto her side so Reggie could get at her tied up hands. He pulled limply at the knots for several minutes, loosening them. Teal pulled her arms free the moment there was slack in the rope. She sat up and started on her legs.

Reggie lay back, his head swimming.

"I'm going to kill those sewer dwelling pricks, Reggie. I'm going to kill every last one of them and then I'm going to kill that damn Esper who tried to get into our heads."

"Tried to get into yours, got into ours." Reggie wiped his face. "I'm still loopy—weak. The others," he looked over at them.

Teal pulled the last of the rope away, flinging it into the corner. "Yeah. Not cool. Super not cool."

Groaning, Reggie pushed himself into a sitting position. "We'd better make sure they're okay. Hopefully whatever that woman did will wear off soon and we can figure out a way to get out of here." He checked his comm-band, but it was gone.

"They took it. They took all our stuff." Teal rubbed her wrists where she had been bound.

"Makes sense." Reggie stood and shuffled over to Emerson. "Help me out."

Teal grunted, her fists clenched. "Yeah, fine." She went over to Azikiwe and crouched down next to her. "Hey. I can't connect to her implant." She bolted up. "I can't connect to my implant!"

Reggie had Emerson on her side and was checking the girl's pulse. "Must be blocking it. Do it the old-fashioned way."

"I'm going to kill that witch, Reggie. Give her

the dead," Teal said through gritted teeth.

"I understand. For now, let's check our people." Reggie opened Emerson's eye, searching for pupil dilation, but struggled in the darkness. He moved on to Dollard as Teal went to Hoa. He got to Muller first and when he finished checking the soldier, went over to where Teal was sitting against the wall.

"All present and accounted for, Captain," Teal said.

"Yeah, I think they just need to sleep it off. I wonder why you could fight it."

"Because I'm awesome." She nudged him with her elbow. "But seriously. No idea. You held on okay."

Reggie huffed. "Better get some sleep while we can."

"Yeah."

THE NEON HEART

SIXTEEN
THE VISITOR

Reggie felt a scuttling across his hand and sat up in a jolt. He flicked away a roach and watched it scuttle under the door. He caught the movement of other insects in the room, skulking in the darkness.

He yawned and leaned back against the wall. Teal was snoring, her head on his leg. She rolled over, murmuring something and went back to sleep leaving a small spot on his pants wet with drool.

Shaking his head, Reggie craned his neck to see the rest of the crew. He and Teal had left them on their sides and they looked like they were resting peacefully from his vantage point.

He yawned and considered waking everyone and looking for a way out of their situation when a thin line of light appeared half way up the far wall. Reggie rubbed his eyes and looked again. The horizontal line made a sharp turn and ran down to the floor, seeming to cut the concrete like paper.

The light made another ninety-degree turn back towards where it started and the section of wall opened up towards him like a door. A frigid breeze wafted a plume of snow into the room and the orange glow of a torch replaced the thin bright light.

A robed figure took a step out from behind the partially opened door, the torch in his hand. Reggie got to his feet. He squinted, trying to cut through the last of the Esper's control on his mind, but the scene didn't change.

Reggie caught a glimpse of the stranger's face under the robe. The man, young, maybe the same age as Emerson, scanned the room and turned to leave.

"Wait." Reggie croaked out the word and cleared his throat. "Wait. Help us."

The figure turned and took a step back through the door.

"Please," Reggie said.

The man hesitated. "I can't. I'm sorry."

Reggie straightened. The pitch of the voice was higher than he expected. The robed stranger was just a boy.

The door closed, cutting off the light. Reggie stumbled towards where it had been and checked the wall for a seam or crack, but the rough concrete was solid. He closed his eyes and took a deep breath before checking again. The wall remained solid. Reggie slumped to the floor. The room still felt chilly from the encounter, but roused from sleep after an Esper had been in his head, he couldn't believe that what he saw was real.

Hearing movement, Reggie turned. Emerson was pushing herself up. He went to help her get seated.

"Hey. You alright?"

She nodded and licked her lips. "I think so. That woman—"

"Relax. She got all of us, except Teal. We're safe for now." Reggie gave her arm a squeeze.

"Why is it so cold?" Emerson lazily looked around the room, taking time to stare at each member of the crew.

"It'll warm up soon." Reggie pulled a bunched corner of her jacket out from behind her and zipped it up.

"Is that snow?" Emerson pointed to a small pile that had blown into a corner.

Reggie turned his head to see. He nodded. "We had a visitor, but he had to go." He looked back to the girl. "Are you good right now? I'm going to go wake everyone up so we can figure out how to get out of this room."

She lifted her chin. "Yeah. I'm okay. Do you want me to put up a wall? Try to keep that woman out of our heads?"

"Not yet. I don't want to alert her before we have a plan in place. For now, just relax."

Reggie crawled over to Dollard and gave the man a shake. "Hey, you okay? It's time to get up," he whispered.

The Esper groaned and covered his head with his arm. "What?"

"We got caught by that woman and her group of walking clothes piles and now we're trapped in a concrete room and I need your help to get out of here." Reggie gave him a pat on the side. "Now, up and at 'em."

"Can I get five more minutes?" Dollard rolled to his back and smirked.

"If you're not up in five I'm going to send Teal after you." Reggie smiled back.

Dollard yawned and stretched. "Yeah, yeah."

As Reggie stood to wake the next sleeper, he saw Emerson next to Teal. The woman flailed at Emerson's nudge and yelped a bit of gibberish.

"What the hell, kid," Teal said. "You don't just wake a lady up when she's been locked up in some room in the Wall. That's how you get face punches."

"She's kidding," Reggie said.

"I'm kind of kidding." Teal put her hand out and Emerson helped her get to her feet. "You good, kid?"

"Yeah," Emerson said.

"Good, now go help the Captain wake everyone else up." Teal shook out her hair and stifled a yawn. "Why the hell is there snow in here?"

"Weird Wall stuff," Reggie said. He crouched next to Azikiwe, but the soldier had been woken by the conversation.

"Sir?"

"Time to get up, soldier. We have a room to get out of."

"What weird Wall stuff?" Teal touched the nearest wall. "Like 'Wall, wall', or just 'wall'?"

"Both, kind of." Reggie left Azikiwe and woke up Muller. Emerson went over to wake Hoa.

"You two don't make any sense," Dollard said. He stood and brushed off his long jacket.

"I make perfect sense," Teal said. "It's this place that's gone crazy."

The soldiers got up quickly and stood at attention. Azikiwe saluted. "Sir, what are our orders?"

Reggie waved off the salute. "For now, take a breath and shake off the rest of whatever that Esper did to us. Then we figure out how to get out of here, and how much time we lost."

"And where the hell they took us," Teal said.

Dollard walked over. "There are a lot of them in the surrounding area. I can see tunnels, like a maze—a sewer system, maybe? We're somewhere in the middle of it."

"Whoa, whoa." Reggie put up a hand. "Don't go poking around and alerting that woman."

"I'm not prodding, it's all around us. Out in the open for everyone to see."

"He's right, sir," Hoa said. "They aren't trying to hide it at all. It's almost as if they are broadcasting it."

Teal clenched her fists. "I suppose with that witch on their side, they don't have much to be scared of. It's probably why the Red Gang didn't follow us past the eighth floor."

"It could be a warning," Dollard said. He looked out past the walls at something Reggie couldn't see. "They aren't on edge, but they aren't totally relaxed either. I see some guards, some patrols. Someone, or something is a threat to them."

"Okay." Reggie scratched his chin. "Well, we can't rely on something coming to rescue us. I need everyone's ideas on how we get out of here."

SEVENTEEN
A PLAN

Teal kicked the door and screamed. She slammed her heel into the spot where a handle would be, over and over, her yell shaking with each impact.

"Give it a rest," Dollard said. "No one is listening."

"AT—LEAST—I'M—TRYING—SOMETHING." Teal looked the Esper in the eyes as she kicked out the words.

They had taken turns trying to get someone to come to their room. Dollard and Hoa read as many people as they could and searched for the witch. Emerson had them covered, but none of them could sense anything.

"They don't care. It's as if they are totally under that woman's spell and won't do a thing without her telling them to." Dollard folded his arms and leaned back against the wall.

Reggie went over to Teal and guided her away from the door.

"I could do it if I had my tools. I know I could."

"I know," Reggie said. "But there is no lock and that door is solid enough to hold off all of us at once. We need another idea."

Azikiwe threw up her hands. "We don't have any more ideas. We can't pick a lock without a lock to pick. We can't knock down the door. We can't reach whatever is barring it shut on the other side. We can't get anyone to come into this hallway, let alone open the damn thing. They apparently have the technology to scramble our implants. There are no other exits, not even a vent, and there is nothing in this room we can use for anything!"

"Relax." Reggie pointed at her then turned to the rest of the group. "I know this is bad, but there is a way out. We just have to find it."

"Time," Teal said.

"I know. I can't worry about that until we find our way out of here."

Hoa pushed herself away from the wall. "I may have something."

"Yeah?" Reggie said.

"Dollard. You said there were patrols on the perimeter of this compound."

Dollard nodded. "Pretty far. They seemed to be scouts. A first line."

"I think I found what they are looking out for." Hoa closed her eyes and put out her hand, fingers spread.

"What do you have?" Azikiwe said.

"Not sure. It's big. It's hungry. Digging. I get a strong impulse to dig."

Teal leaned on Reggie's shoulder. "What do we do with this information?"

"I'm not sure," Hoa said. "It's all I've got."

Emerson put up her hand. "I may be able to do something."

Teal raised an eyebrow at the girl. "What?"

"That lady, who controlled us. I think our abilities come from the same place."

"You can control people?" Teal left Reggie and closed in on Emerson.

"Not people. When I was little, I could, kind of, talk with animals." Emerson shook her head. "Not talk, really. I could read them, like any Esper, but I could give them impressions. Ideas. Sometimes it worked, but only on little things."

"I thought you were a blocker?" Reggie said.

"The impressions are an extension of blocking. That's all I can do on people. It's why they picked me up." Emerson looked at the floor. "That's all they focused on in training."

Dollard huffed. "Highly unlikely."

"Unlikely or not, what did you have in mind?"

Reggie asked.

"I don't know. I can try to connect with whatever it is. Suggest it come this way?"

"And you can get it to open the door?" Teal asked.

Emerson shook her head. "I doubt it. If I can even do anything, the best I can guess is to lead it here."

Reggie scratched his chin. "No. That's good. That could help."

Teal spun to face him. "How?"

"Right now, we are stuck in a particular situation and can't seem to have any effect on it. If we get this thing over here, it's going to shake things up. Maybe cause some kind of opportunity." Reggie walked past Teal to Emerson. "See what you can do. Get that thing as close to this room as you can, and if possible, alert as many people as you can."

Emerson nodded and closed her eyes. Reggie turned to Hoa and Dollard.

"You two, keep poking around. If you get any sense of how they're reacting to this thing, let me know. Otherwise, make sure they know you are poking around."

"Sir." Hoa saluted.

Dollard sighed.

"Okay." Reggie went to the rest of the group. "Back to the door. We'll take turns if we have to.

Scream, kick, bash. Make some noise. Maybe we can get the attention of that witch and find a way to get out of here. Be ready to protect the others if they come in hard."

"Hup," Azikiwe and Muller said in unison. They went to the door. Muller kicked while Azikiwe yelled something Reggie couldn't understand without his comm-band interpreting.

Teal pulled Reggie to the far corner of the room. "What do we do if that lady shuts you all down again?" she yelled over the noise.

"I'm sure you'll think of something."

"You don't have anything for her, do you?"

"I have a fully trained operative who seems to be immune to her ability."

"And what the hell am I supposed to do against however many hundred of those people there are out there?"

"That's what the distraction is for."

Teal stared at him with her mouth open.

"Hey, you were the one who said I don't use my resources effectively."

"Wait." Teal smiled and punched him in the arm. "Was that a joke?"

"I don't know what you're talking about."

"This is a terrible plan, but I'm totally taking credit for getting you to tell a joke in the middle of it."

"Just make some noise, Teal." Reggie walked over to Emerson.

"That's what I'm doing!" Teal screamed and jumped up and down. "Hey you stupid lady who made my crew fall asleep. Come get some!"

Reggie crouched next to Emerson. "How's it going?"

"I think it's coming. It didn't need too much prodding. Like Hoa said, it's hungry. It already knows these people are here. I just gave it the impression that it should come here to hunt."

"And it listened?"

"I wouldn't say listened. It liked the idea. It's moving this way. Fast."

"Good work." Reggie started to stand, but Emerson grabbed onto his sleeve.

"Sir, wait."

Reggie stopped. "What is it?"

"I'm not controlling this thing. It's coming, but I don't know what it's going to do, or where it will end up. I can't make it do anything." She wrinkled her forehead. "It's really big and it'll be here really soon."

Reggie squeezed her arm. "Okay. I understand. Keep an eye on it. If you can get it to end up close to the room, do it."

EIGHTEEN
A WAY OUT

Reggie replaced Muller at the door. They focused their kicks in the same spot. He hoped that if their plan didn't work, whatever kept it locked would give way. Teal had run out of things to call their captors and switched to yelling nursery rhymes. Azikiwe and Muller stood in fighting positions in case someone came in and the Espers kept at their tasks of disruption and luring.

Dollard and Emerson got to their feet at the same time. Reggie gave up kicking and breathed heavily. He put a hand on Teal's shoulder to get her to stop screaming Humpty Dumpty.

"What is it?"

"It's here," Emerson said.

Dollard looked to the door. "So are they, and they are upset."

Hoa stood, her eyes wide. "Upset. They're

pissed."

She and Dollard stared at the same spot at the wall, near where the robbed figure had appeared to Reggie.

"Holy shit." Dollard covered his face.

"That thing is pissed too!" Hoa said.

The wall burst outward at them, sending chunks of concrete and a plume of dirt raining down on them. The giant head of a mutated something came into the room. Its yellow, chipped buckteeth were the size of Reggie's arm. It screeched and pushed its snout further towards them. Globs of mucus hanging off of the black nose dripped into the foaming drool leaking from its maw.

It widened the opening, extending an arm tipped with sharp, flat claws, reaching towards the group.

Teal jumped back, away from the grasping sweep as Muller and Azikiwe ducked under it.

"Get back," Reggie yelled, pulling Emerson behind him. He turned to the door and gave it another kick. "Hey, get us out of here!" His jacket shifted colour to blend in with the grey walls.

Over the snarl of the beast, he heard voices behind the metal slab.

"Hey!" He booted it again and Teal came over to pull him away.

"Focus. Biggest problem." She spun him to face the monster.

He grimaced. "Right. Emerson, Dollard. Back here. Work on the door. Everyone else, spread out, don't give it a direction to go. Keep changing its focus."

The soldiers let out a 'hup' and evenly spaced themselves across the room with Teal and Reggie in the middle.

Muller jumped towards the giant mole. The foul snout sniffed at him and the arm followed. He pulled back, the claws cutting the air where he had been with a whoosh.

Positioned on the opposite side, Hoa lunged. She punched the mole on the side of the face and rolled under the responding swing, giving Azikiwe an opportunity to strike.

"They aren't going to do any damage to this thing with their fists," Teal said before jumping in to distract it.

"Yeah." Reggie glanced around the room, his attention darting back to the creature with every move it made. He spotted the concrete rubble and grabbed the closest piece. It was about the size of a lumpy potato, and as heavy. Chucking it at the mole, he grabbed for another piece.

"Now you're talking," Muller said. The soldier found a large chunk and swung it at the beast, drawing its focus. Azikiwe threw more rubble and Hoa found a large piece like Muller.

Reggie dug into the dirt, looking for more ammunition and cut his hand on something sharp. He winced and pulled away, holding the injury close. The cut wasn't deep, but it started to bleed immediately. He went back to the mound more cautiously and pulled out a reinforcing rod sheared off to about three feet. A piece of concrete clung to the opposite end of the sharp point. Waiting for an opportunity, Reggie slipped forward, and ducked under the flailing arm of the beast. He swung up with the rebar, breaking off the rocky end on the mole's jaw.

It snarled and snapped at him but he managed to deflect the nasty teeth with the metal. Muller jumped over him, bludgeoning the monster on top of its head. More debris clattered to the floor as the concrete crumbled.

Reggie rolled out of range as Hoa stepped in to give Muller an escape.

The creature managed to snag Muller by his chest piece and pulled him towards its face.

Hoa screamed and swung her concrete boulder at the monster over and over again. "Let him go!"

Reggie got to a knee and saw the beast bury its teeth into Muller's leg. The soldier screamed and tried to force the creature's mouth open.

"Muller!" Reggie pushed around Hoa to get into the man's line of sight. He tossed the rebar and the soldier caught it, plunging it deep into the monster's eye.

It screeched, dropping Muller, and scrambled with its clawed arm to get the metal spike out of its head. Flailing, it smashed its other arm into the room and swung it wildly at the group, keeping them back.

Teal and Reggie ran to Muller. He was holding his shredded leg. Blood spurted out in gouts with each beat of his heart. It mixed with the dirt on the floor, creating red mud that clung to them.

Moving Muller's hands away from the wound, Teal pulled at a punctured and twisted armor plate, but it was embedded into his leg.

"Shit. Reggie. I can't get this free."

"Hang on, Muller. This is going to hurt." Reggie rolled the soldier onto his side. Muller grunted at the movement.

"I need a knife, or something that can cut through this material."

"They took everything," Teal said.

Reggie wiped his face. "Okay. Do your best to stem the bleeding."

Getting into a crouch, Reggie watched the mutated creature. Its focus was on the rebar as it struggled to get it free. Its other arm swung randomly into the room. Hoa and Azikiwe danced around it, peppering the monster with debris in retaliation for their injured squad member.

When the monster swiped a claw at them, Reggie bolted for its face. Its foul snout sniffed and turned towards him. Skidding in the dirt, he stopping just short of snapping teeth. He jumped to the side to avoid a bloody claw and clambered over it to reach the metal bar. As soon as he touched it, the giant mole shrieked and flung him back with its big front paw. Claws scrapped across his jacket, but the material withstood the sharp nails.

Reggie landed near Teal and Muller, the gore covered rebar in his hand. He struggled to catch his breath and handed the sharp metal rod to Teal.

"Go." He coughed and held his shoulder.

Teal nodded and went back to Muller. She used the rebar to cut away the resistant material holding the armor plate to the soldier's leg.

The creature, injured but the metal removed its eye, refocused on its attack. It used its free arms to pull itself farther into the room.

Reggie got back to his feet and sighed. "Maybe this was a bad idea."

The door to the room opened and the small, heavily clothed figures poured in. Dollard pushed Emerson behind the door and the Espers hugged the wall.

Reggie spotted his pistol and at least one of the soldier's rifles among the myriad of weapons in the hands of the small sewer dwellers. Hoa and Azikiwe split their attention between the new threat and the monster still encroaching into the room.

Behind the dozens of figures, the woman who had captured them stepped into the doorway. She wore a necklace made of collected trinkets. Reggie saw his comm-band and the soldiers' dog tags among the dozens of other small items hanging low on the woman's chest.

She looked like a svelte giant towering over her small slaves—a twisted Snow White and her warped dwarves.

"What is the meaning—" Her booming voice was cut short when she saw the creature, huge and leaking foul fluids. It snatched up two of her zombie-like followers and pulled them into its mouth.

Jumping to her feet, Teal pushed her way through the cluster of small cloth-covered hostiles, the rebar in hand. Before the Esper woman could react, Teal attacked. She drove the metal spear down through the woman's shoulder and out her back. The witch collapsed into a heap. Without direct control, her followers went wild. Some seemed to shut down, like automatons cut from their power source. Others attacked the nearest enemy. The ones closest to the mutant creature focused on the obvious threat, firing their weapons and retreating.

Reggie saw Teal pull the rebar free and swing it at the dwellers surrounding her. His attention was drawn to the five cloth-people aiming their weapons at Muller and him. He dove at the nearest one, easily dragging it to the ground. He wrestled its old blaster free, a relic that fired big cartridge rounds, and shot the other four assailants. Before he could get back to Muller, Hoa bounded over the milling figures in the middle of the room and planted herself in front of him. She held one of their modern rifles and exchanged shots with the dwellers she had jumped over. Reggie threw the blaster to Muller, who did his best to help Hoa, and grabbed his pistol from one of the cloth mounds he'd shot.

"Time to go," he yelled over the frenzy. He moved towards Teal to help her, but she had already dispatched the zealots who attempted to avenge their fallen leader and confiscated an older mark one rifle. She was crouching over the female Esper, going through the things hanging around her neck. They both made it to Dollard and Emerson, helping the Espers escape to the hallway.

Reggie stopped at the doorway. Hoa was holding her side, the onslaught from the remaining enemies not fighting the mole getting through her armor. Muller wasn't moving, either dead or unconscious from the loss of blood. Azikiwe was fighting her way towards them.

"Come on!" Reggie stepped back into the room, trying to clear a path for the soldiers. Azikiwe spotted him and made her way over, but Hoa kept fighting.

Reggie watched a shot snap her head back. She slumped backwards over Muller, half of her face gone. He pulled Azikiwe with him into the hallway and they ran after Teal and the Espers.

THE NEON HEART

NINETEEN
RUN

With Azikiwe covering their retreat, she and Reggie caught up to the others. Teal, Dollard and Emerson were stopped at an intersection of tunnels.

"Hoa? Muller?" Teal asked.

Reggie shook his head, catching his breath.

"They went down fighting." Azikiwe kept her rifle trained down the hallway where they had come from.

Teal let the soldiers' dog tags dangle out of her hand. "Here. I snagged these off that witch after I jammed that metal rod down her idiot throat."

Azikiwe put them around her neck and sniffed.

"We've got to go," Reggie said between ragged breaths. He pointed at the Espers. "You two glean anything about where we are while you were digging around in their heads"

Emerson was trembling. She didn't look at him.

"No."

Dollard reached his hand out. "I can tell where they aren't. Based on where their patrols were going, I'd say this is a way out and the majority of them are behind us."

"Good. Let's go." Reggie took the lead. Teal tossed him his comm-band as he slipped past her. He put it on and the contacts and speaker patch behind his ear connected.

He could see a readout of their status, streamed from their implants, reactivated amidst the chaos. Projected over his path, he could see signs of stress in their readings. Heart rate and blood pressure was up across the board, except for the flat lines of Hoa and Muller.

The passageway shrank and Reggie had to duck. He moved at a light run, checking behind him to make sure the rest of his squad was keeping up.

The tunnel opened into a large round room with no floor. A catwalk ran around the wall, rusted like the grates they passed when they were being dragged into the complex. On the opposite side was a large concrete pipe that continued in the same direction, nearly as large as the hallway. The ceiling of the room was low, but Reggie didn't have to duck as he stepped onto the walkway. It groaned under his weight and shook as he walked. At the halfway point, it pulled away from the wall and creaked, threatening to collapse. He stopped and Emerson ran into him. He stumbled and fell to his knees, the Esper leaning over him.

Reggie heard Teal wince as the section of the catwalk he was on dropped a foot, stopping with a screech and shutter. In a single motion, Reggie stood, pulling Emerson with him, and jumped to the next section.

"Other way!" he yelled as the walkway started to fall like dominos from the sunken section. Dragging Emerson, Reggie ran to the pipe and pushed her in before him.

Dollard, Azikiwe, and Teal ran around the other side of the wall. The sections of the catwalk tumbled into the dark pit behind them.

Reggie stretched out as far as he could, trying to will them to reach him. He strained, groaning like the remains of the rusty metal. Dollard was close, the women right behind him. Reggie was focused on their desperate charge and didn't see the cluster of cloth covered figures at the other opening. They fired across the chasm, driving Reggie back and nearly hitting the frantic runners on the collapsing catwalk.

Dropping to a knee, Reggie fired back. One of the heaps of clothing collapsed as he shot it. The act drew their fire. Dollard, Azikiwe, and Teal had nearly reached him. Ignoring the echo of their assorted weapons, he grabbed Dollard by his outstretched arm and pulled him into the pipe. Azikiwe slipped by Reggie before he could help her and immediately started to return fire. Reggie leaned out to help Teal and the last section of the walkway fell.

Teal screamed as the floor below her gave way. She grasped at the tunnel, but her hands slipped on the concrete. Reggie grabbed at her, crashing to his stomach. He let go of his pistol and caught her wrist, squeezing as hard as he could. He managed to keep his grip as she careened off the wall of the pit, but her momentum pulled him with her. He spread his legs, trying to wedge himself in the pipe, but couldn't stop himself from slipping.

The sewer dwellers kept firing above him, but he and Teal were obvious and helpless targets.

Before he went over the edge, he felt hands grab his ankles. He wasn't being pulled up, but his descent had stopped.

"Get up here. You two are heavy," Azikiwe said.

Teal's gaze darted frantically in every direction. Reggie tried to make eye contact, but she kept looking away.

"Hey! Get it together." A shot from the sewer dwellers hit a section of the curved wall next to Reggie, sending debris flecking his face. "Teal, now!"

The dangling operative looked up at Reggie. Her face was pale and her expression vacant.

"Okay. Now, you need to climb up to the pipe and help the others pull me in."

Teal nodded.

"Good. On my mark, I'm going to pull. You have to grab on to me and start climbing. Got it?"

She nodded again.

"What's going on down there?" Azikiwe said, straining.

"I'm going to pull and send her up. Get ready?" Another chunk of wall was blasted away near his leg, making Reggie twitch. "Go!"

Reggie pulled as hard as he could. He brought Teal up towards him, but the action caused him to slip farther down the wall. She grabbed onto his clothes and leg and scaled him. Her weight lessened as she reached the top and clambered into the opening. When she was safe, he felt himself being pulled up after her.

A flurry of shots cascaded above him and he heard a yelp. One of the pairs of hands on his ankles let go and he slid back down. Someone else grabbed him and he stopped with a jolt. A bullet grazed his leg and he yelled.

"Drop me a gun!" Reggie felt the spot where the bullet hit him. His hand came away red, but the wound was small.

"Kind of busy," Teal said through clenched teeth.

"We're gonna get eaten alive like this."

"Hey," Emerson called from the tunnel opening.

Reggie looked up. The Esper held out Azikiwe's rifle. "Perfect. Drop it."

Emerson let the rifle go. It came at him faster than he expected and bounced off his outstretched hand. It hit his back and rolled to his other side. He grabbed it by the barrel before it fell out of reach and sighed. Another bullet from the cloth heaps across the pit drew his attention back to the moment. Pushing himself off the wall with one hand, he aimed with the other and fired a spread into the far tunnel.

Two of the dwellers fell, disappearing into the darkness below. The others retreated.

With the threat halted, Reggie felt himself being pulled into the passageway.

"Who got hit?" Reggie asked as he scooted away from the pit.

"I did, sir," Azikiwe said. "Clean through the shoulder. I'll be fine."

Reggie handed her the rifle. "Thank you."

"Where were you hit?" Teal patted him in random spots.

He brushed her off of him. "Grazed in the leg. Nothing some disinfectant can't fix."

"Hey." Azikiwe tossed him a spray bottle. Emerson was wrapping her shoulder.

"Where'd you get that?"

Teal slapped it out of his hand and grinned at him. "I took it off that woman. Thanks for catching me."

"Thanks for making me have to pick up the bottle, I guess." Reggie picked up the spray.

Dollard shuffled around Emerson and Azikiwe. "No time to rest. We have to go."

"Hold on." Reggie sprayed his leg and winced. "We don't even know where we are. We should get our bearings first."

"I know where we are." Dollard looked behind him, farther down the pipe. "It's not a good place to be."

THE NEON HEART

TWENTY
FROM BELOW

Reggie took a piece of cloth that Teal had torn off her shirt and tied it around his leg. "Okay, Dollard. What's going on?"

"There's no time." Dollard balled up his fists and put them to his temple. "In the pit—so many of them. We woke them up."

"We woke up what?" Teal zipped up her jacket.

"Don't know and we don't want to find out. They are vicious—hungry. They're coming."

"That's good enough for me," Reggie said. "What are we looking at for weapons?"

Azikiwe held up her rifle. "It's been banged around a bit, but I've got a mostly full charge, minus that suppression you laid down on those cloth people."

Teal crossed her arms. "I had some kind of old something-or-other, but I dropped it when I fell."

"And I lost my pistol." Reggie nodded towards the pit. He looked at Dollard and Emerson. "Any chance one of you grabbed something?"

"That was not my first instinct." Dollard sneered and looked away. "We don't have time for this."

"I took this from one of them," Emerson said. She held a knife with a blade about the size of her small hand. It had faint carvings on the surface and a gem set into the end of the hilt.

"It's better than nothing." Reggie took it and tossed it to Teal. "You're better with a blade than I am."

"If you wanted me to take the lead so badly, all you had to do was ask." Teal winked, grinning.

"Yeah, well." Reggie shrugged. "Take the lead. Azikiwe, cover our back. Let's go."

"Finally." Dollard rushed down the large pipe, making the rest of them jog to catch up.

Reggie kept the Espers in between himself and Teal. He sidled up to Dollard. "Anything else you can tell me about what's in the pit?"

"No. I told you everything." Dollard clenched his jaw and kept looking forward.

"What about ahead of us? Any impressions?"

"Captain. I'm sure you don't know much about Espers, but when there is a threat as consuming as the one behind us, it's not easy to block it out and lazily scan the huge network of tunnels and hallways in front of us. We are not computers."

"Right. I suppose I don't have to tell you to let me know if you do feel something?" Reggie left Dollard and caught up with Teal.

She held the knife out, ready to strike in the dark passage. "He give you anything other than attitude?"

"Just reemphasized how bad the thing behind us is." Reggie glanced back.

"Don't believe him?"

"I have no doubt we should be afraid of something that lives in a pit in the Wall. I just need info about what's in front of us, not behind. We have to figure out where we are if we are going to get to The Neon Heart."

Teal looked up and away, checking something with her implant. "You check the time since you got that comm-band back?"

Reggie sighed. "Yeah. Between our capture, being locked up, and that escape, we lost about ten hours. Unless those cloth-heaps dragged us in the right direction, we aren't going to make it."

"Yeah." Teal smacked the flat of the knife against her palm.

"I'm not giving up, but…" Reggie put his hand on Teal's shoulder. She shrugged it off. "I'm sorry about Muller and Hoa."

Teal didn't look at him. "They were good soldiers. I worked with them a lot. Always reliable, no

153

freak-outs, none of that rage that makes some of them so vicious. They were smart." She shook her head. "You know me. I don't like letting my crew get too close, but I ended up relying on them, Reg."

Reggie scratched his chin.

"I know. I shouldn't have expected to get out of this one without casualties. I just thought, with this group. We were special. Made it out of tough scrapes before." Teal let her arm drop to her side. "Thanks for not saying it."

"Yeah."

"Something else on your mind?" Teal nudged him.

"It's my fault." Reggie clicked his tongue. "Not like woe-is-me." He frowned. "It's my mission. My timetable. My reward. Even if they all signed up for their own reason, it's tough to shake."

Dollard stepped up behind them. "Would you two get moving? I can feel those things getting closer."

Teal waved him off with the knife. "He's right. Time to focus."

"Yeah. Priority one, get out of danger—this danger. Next, we figure out where we are."

Teal picked up the pace and Reggie fell back with the Espers. He looked back to Azikiwe.

"Anything?"

"Not yet, sir." The soldier kept her rifle trained

at the darkness.

"I'm sorry about your—"

"With all due respect. Not the time, sir," she said.

Reggie pressed his lips together and nodded to himself. Up ahead, he saw the end of the pipe.

"Here we go," Teal said.

The passage led to a square room with a ladder bolted to the far wall. It went up through a round tube formed out of the concrete wall and ceiling. A dull bulb cast a pale yellow light from a fixture against the wall, failing to illuminate the whole space.

Reggie stood straight and stretched his neck. "That's a little better. I guess, up we go."

"On it," Teal said. She put the knife in her mouth and started to climb. She reached the spot where the ladder continued into the ceiling and stopped. "I can see some really small spots of light up there. No idea what's at the top, but it's a loooong climb." She mumbled the words past the knife and continued up the ladder.

"Anywhere is going to be better than here when those things catch up to us." Dollard rushed to the ladder and followed Teal. "Come on!"

"Alright. You next," Reggie said to Emerson.

The girl didn't respond, but followed the order.

"Now you, sir," Azikiwe said.

"Here. Give me the rifle. You should go next."

The soldier pulled the gun away from Reggie's

reach. "You're acting on guilt. I'll do my job, thank you."

Reggie grimaced. "You're right. Sorry." He went to the ladder but stopped at the first rung. The sound of rapid tapping wafted from the pipe. "Did you hear that?"

Azikiwe kneeled and raised the rifle. "I did. Hurry."

"Let's go. I want you a step behind me on this ladder. No last stands." The sound got louder. Reggie caught movement in the darkness. The walls looked like they were undulating.

Backing away, Azikiwe shot into the moving mass. The flashes of light showed a wave of cock-roach-looking insects the size of Reggie's hand. They coated the sides of the pipe and skittered towards them like rushing water.

Reggie jumped off the ladder and grabbed Azikiwe by the armor plate on her back and pulled her away from the chittering bugs. "Too many, too fast!" He grabbed the rungs and climbed as quickly as he could. In the darkness above, he could just make out the shape of Emerson.

"Better move it up there! There are hundreds of them."

TWENTY ONE
HUNDREDS

"Hundreds of what?" Teal called down, the knife still obscuring the words.

"Big bugs." Reggie skipped rungs, catching up to the others.

"Wait. How big?"

"Will fist-sized roaches make you climb faster?" Reggie heard his words reverberate in the concrete tube.

"Shit. Yes!"

Reggie reached Emerson and willed her to move faster. "Come on. They are right behind us." He looked down and saw a circle of pale yellow light from the square room. Azikiwe looked like a shadow a few feet below him. She kept her rifle in hand, slowing her progress.

Around the shape of the soldier, he saw the bugs. They reached the ladder and skittered behind it, up the walls. When they reached the tube, they spread to coat the interior. The sound of their legs on the concrete and what he guessed were pincers clacking seemed to surround them.

"Move!" Reggie grabbed the rungs as Emerson's feet lifted off, but the insects were so much faster.

Over the sound of them advancing, he heard Azikiwe open fire. She shot in bursts, cutting through swaths of the black bugs, leaving pockmarks on the walls. For every one she hit, more filled in the space. Reggie saw them continue to cross the section of floor he could see, piling on top of each other as they scrambled after his group.

"Ah! These pricks bite." Azikiwe stopped to brush them off of her. She switched from shooting to bashing the bugs with her rifle.

"Don't slow down. They'll overwhelm you." The first few who had passed Azikiwe reached Reggie. He kicked at them, squishing some into globs of pus and innards, but as soon as one was killed, more took its place. Some jumped onto him, biting at his jacket, searching for a way in. Others passed him, nipping at Emerson.

Reggie slapped at the roaches as he climbed, trying to keep them from biting the Esper. "How much farther? They're on us."

"Not far now. Few metres," Teal mumbled.

One of the bugs chomped at Reggie's wounded

leg, cutting through his pants and the makeshift bandage. He tried to squish it, but it seemed unfazed by his attack and bit deeper into his cut. He screamed and knocked it free with a flurry of swings. He looked down and saw that Azikiwe had fallen behind. The soldier was covered in bugs.

They swarmed her injured shoulder and clung to her between her armor plates. She stopped trying to get them off and went back to shooting—holding the trigger down. The bugs coated the walls several layers deep where she was. Each bullet annihilated clusters of the insects as more poured in and up the tube after them. She screamed and let out guttural roars that peaked over the clicking echoing in the tube and off the shiny black carapaces of the insects.

"Climb!" Reggie yelled down to her. "Just keep climbing!" He let go of the rung and slid down the side rails. The insects he knocked free on his rapid descent rained down to the bottom and joined the others still charging into the tube.

Reggie tried to get next to Azikiwe in the small space, but she was almost completely covered in the big roaches. She had stopped shooting and flailed under the onslaught. Her screams were replaced with frantic yelps and moans. Reggie pulled bugs from her, but there were too many. Each one came away with chunks of flesh. They jumped to him, clustering around his wound and spreading out to cover his legs. Pincers tore through his pants and gouged at him.

"Come on. Ignore them and climb!" He yelled over the cacophonous sound of clicking and tried to grab hold of the soldier's wrist to guide her up. As soon as he took some of her weight, she slipped from the ladder. Reggie nearly dropped her as he took the full burden of the Azikiwe and her gear. A bug bit his hand and he almost let go.

"Hey! Don't give up," Reggie said through clenched teeth. The dangling body managed to block some of the bugs, but they continued to swarm him, prodding him, seeking a way in. She stopped moving, but the blood that sprayed onto his hand, making it slick, pulsed from her rhythmically with the beating of her heart.

Sudden light poured in at the top of the ladder, mirroring the insects still rising from the pipe below. Reggie heard screams from above, but couldn't make out what the others were saying.

"Azikiwe!" Taking a deep breath, Reggie pulled on the arm and stepped up a rung on the ladder. He felt a rending and worried his grip would give. Hooking an elbow though the ladder, he used both hands to pull Azikiwe up by her wrist. He managed to get her hand to a rung and tried to guide her fingers to grab hold, but the rest of her body dropped. Reggie nearly fell after her as his feet slipped from the ladder. His elbow was wrenched, but he ignored the sharp pain. As Azikiwe's body tumbled to the floor, knocking away a cascade of roaches as it fell, he still held on to her arm.

A convulsion of vomit gurgled into his throat, but he held it back. He squeezed his eyes shut and dropped her arm. A sharp bite on his ankle got him moving. Reggie let the insects chew on him and scrambled up the ladder as quickly as he could. The sound of them below chased him as he surged towards the circle of light. He saw Teal leaning over the opening, her arm stretched towards him. As fast as he was going, the insects were faster. They climbed the walls around him as he reached the top. Teal grabbed his jacket and pulled as he flung himself out of the tube and onto the floor. He heard a slam as the cover was dropped back into place.

The roaches that made it out in time skittered away from the light. Teal and Emerson helped Reggie pull free the ones who were reluctant to give up their purchase on his arms and legs. The bugs that weren't squished joined the others who had run towards the shadows.

"Azikiwe." Reggie shuddered, trying to catch his breath. He groaned as Teal helped him sit up and pulled his jacket off. She stripped off his shirt and pants, evicting the last few roaches and exposing their damage. His head swam and he swayed.

"Shut up and let me see—" Teal put her hand over her mouth. "Oh god, Reggie. They did a number on you."

"Her arm. She fell"

"Yeah, I know. We saw what happened. I'll convince you it's not your fault later. For now I need to stop you from bleeding to death." Teal used his shirt to clean out his wounds. Pain spiked though him as she dug into the gashes the bugs had gouged into him.

"You may as well go ahead and pass out. This isn't going to get any easier." Teal reached behind her and Emerson handed her the spray bottle of antiseptic.

Reggie lay back onto the cold floor, closed his eyes, and took her advice.

TWENTY TWO
A SMARTER
MOVE

Reggie opened his eyes and blinked against the bright, buzzing light. His jacket was draped over him like a blanket. He sat up and felt his stiff muscles strain against the movement. Grunting, he propped himself against the nearest wall. He was in some kind of storage room with half-broken shelves running along one side. An old boiler in the corner took up a quarter of the room. Teal was standing by a closed door, Emerson and Dollard sitting near her on the dirty floor.

"Hey, look who's awake." Teal held out his torn and stained shirt. "Cute top. Had to use some of it to bandage you up." She pulled her coat open to show her bare stomach. "I started to run out."

"Awesome. My pants?" Reggie checked the small strips of fabric tied around his arms and legs. He winced as he stood.

"Fared a little better. I tried to pin the worst holes closed, but we have limited resources on hand." Teal tossed the pants at Reggie and he slipped them on.

"Thanks. How are we looking?" Putting on the remains of his shirt, Reggie slipped his arm through the wrong hole.

"Do you want the good news, the bad news, or the worse news?"

"There's some good news?"

Teal went over and helped Reggie put his jacket on. "By some twisted fluke, we are actually pretty close to the Heart. We're on the right level and everything."

"How do you know that?"

Teal pointed to a map tacked up on the wall. A spider web of tunnels and corridors twisted around and over each other, levels depicted as separate webs next to each other. "It looks like this was a maintenance room that served some complex and transportation system. If we're here," she pointed to a spot on the map, "then the Heart is over here." She traced a path through the spaghetti to a point at the edge. Written in blue marker someone had scrawled 'Heart'. Next to it in red, a cartoon heart was drinking from a tankard.

"Does the bad news have anything to do with three casualties?" Reggie stretched, cracking his neck and shoulder. His muscles ached.

Shaking her head, Teal leaned against the wall next to him. "For one. We're low on time."

Reggie checked his comm-band. The countdown he had started back on the space station was down to under three hours. He scratched his head. "And?"

"Between us and the Heart is… Well, it's not good."

"It doesn't matter. We're abandoning the mission." Reggie checked the sync between his comm-band, patch, and contacts. When the link was verified, he tried to find a signal relay where he could send a message to the Director.

"What?" Teal smacked his arm with the back of her hand, hitting a spot where the insects had taken a bite out of him.

Reggie grimaced. "Ouch. We are down three people and out of time. There is no reason to take any more risks."

"I don't think you have a good handle on the situation there, buck-o." Teal crossed her arms.

"No. I think I just explained it pretty succinctly." Reggie pressed against the patch behind his ear, making sure the conductive speaker was well attached.

"How do you expect us to get out of here? We can't go back the way we came."

"We'll find another way out. There has to be a

stairwell close by. We find it and start climbing."

"How long before we run into some freaks like the ones who captured us? Or stumble back into the Red Gang territory?" Teal paced around the small room, punctuating her comments with wild hand gestures.

"Trying to get to The Neon Heart with no soldiers and no weapons is suicide. I'd rather take my chance—"

"Wandering around this maze for another day, or two? Week? Risking running into god-knows-what? That's a much smarter move."

Reggie reached down to scratch his leg and the gashes on his arm and torso flared like fire. He gritted his teeth and straightened. "Teal!"

"What!" She flung her arms over her head.

Reggie took a deep breath. "I'm not going to argue. We're in this mess because that stupid thing they have in the Heart is the ticket to everything I've always wanted. I don't need any more people to die for my petty little reward."

Teal stomped over to him and pushed him against the wall. "You self-centered ass. We're all getting something for this job, you dumb-idiot. Do you think we're all here because we like you? I'm convinced Dollard would hand you back to those cloth-heaps if he thought it would get him out of here."

"I wouldn't," Dollard said.

Teal spun, pointing at Dollard. "Of course you wouldn't. They'd just kill you too. That's not the point." She turned back to Reggie. "I'm doing this because it means Amcoral is going to offer me a huge contract to get me away from Telbak when this thing is over. I'm going to be able to skip middle management and get a cushy junior executive position out of this. So, don't you dare take the moral high-ground. That was my squad we lost. This mission is as much all of ours as it is yours and we're not your frail entourage who needs you to protect us or give up your precious dreams for our safety—especially when there is no safety to be found down here."

Reggie opened his mouth to reply, but Teal pushed him again.

"I'm not finished. I'm just calming down so I don't yell the next part!" Teal kept her finger in his face.

Reggie put up his hands and shrugged. It hurt.

"Good." Teal put her finger down. "Now. Like I said, we are close to the Heart. There are some things in our way and we are without the benefit of soldiers, but I'd argue that getting to The Neon Heart and using the elevator to escape, dealing with a known threat, is a tactically smarter move than wandering around in this death-trap."

"You done?" Reggie clenched his jaw.

"Depends on what you say next."

"You're right. I'm sorry."

Teal huffed and took a step back. "That wasn't so hard."

Reggie stared at her.

Teal shrugged and looked away. "Okay, finish."

"Between us and the Heart is their security guarding a buffer zone, Consortium troopers with who-knows-what kind of armaments, and whatever it was that you were reluctant to tell me. If we can get into the place, we will still have to find the device, then hope that we can access the elevator, where, at the top will be more Consortium soldiers waiting for us."

"Can I talk again?"

"Go ahead," Reggie said.

"Whatever security a dive bar in the middle of the Wall has may keep the riffraff at bay, but I doubt they will be enough to handle two operatives. As for the Consortium, okay, you got me there. But even with a shadow organization backing them, they still have limited resources. I doubt they have the kind of training we do."

"And?"

"And what?"

Reggie gestured to the wall. "What about the still unnamed menace between us and them."

"To be honest, I don't know. It's something our

Esper friends over there sensed in the area. One of countless unknown perils we would face wandering around in the Wall, looking for another way out. Plus, that option precludes us from finishing our job."

Reggie rubbed his chin. "You've successfully convinced me that both options are terrible." He walked past her to the Espers still sitting against the far wall. "Anything to add?"

Dollard looked away, sneering. "I would not turn anyone over to any of the gangs and I am insulted at the insinuation."

"To speak for Teal, she was just explaining to me that you don't care for me and would just as soon had me not survive over Azikiwe, Hoa, or Muller."

"I'll admit to that."

"Good." Reggie stopped himself from rolling his eyes. "Now, what about our options?"

"I'm with Teal. I'd much rather take a risk to get out of here faster and have an opportunity to fulfill my contract." Dollard stood. "I'm not a physical man, but I am no coward. I'm a trained Telbak Esper, top of the ranks. I've been in bad situations before."

"I wouldn't call you a coward, Dollard. Not after what we've been through." Reggie clapped him on the shoulder and looked down at Emerson. "What about you?"

She turned away. "I want to finish the job."

"Are you sure?"

She looked at him, her expression stoic. "I have a lot riding on this mission, too. If there is a chance I can get you to the Heart, we have to try."

Reggie sighed. "That's three to one. I'm convinced. It would be nice to have some weapons, but we'll have to improvise."

"We've been there before." Teal tapped the knife against the palm of her hand. "I'm less concerned with whatever security The Neon Heart has than whatever Dollard is reading between them and us."

"What are we looking at?" Reggie gingerly zipped up his jacket.

"It's big. Too big to reasonably fit down here," Dollard said.

"So it's something that's from the Wall. That grew here."

"Sure." Dollard fluttered his eyes. "It's hard to read. If it has a consciousness it's fragmented. It's angry though. It radiates from it."

"And you can't tell what it is?"

"No." Dollard sneered.

Emerson stood. "It's not like most creatures. Usually you can get a sense of intelligence or some kind of animal instinct. From what you read, you can piece together a sense of what something is. This thing—"

"It's not something either of us have ever sensed, or seen, before," Dollard said.

Reggie took a deep breath. "Right. Malevolent mystery monster."

"That's not all. There are other, smaller things. Not as dangerous, but still animalistic. We should be wary of them too."

"Okay. Thanks." Reggie turned to face the door. He pointed to his left and looked over his shoulder at Dollard. The Esper nodded. "Only option I see is to run. Get through this thing's territory as quickly as we can and hope The Neon Heart's security keep it contained. Once we get there, Teal and I can carve a path through them and whatever Consortium help they have."

"Hell yeah, we can." Teal said.

"The important thing is to stick together. I don't want to lose any of you to heroics or negligence. We watch each other's backs, and move as a unit."

Teal snickered. "Unit."

"Thank you, Teal." Reggie grimaced. "Is everybody ready?"

"What about you?" Teal asked.

"I'll be fine."

"No heroics." She pointed at her eyes and back to him.

Emerson waved Reggie over to where she was standing by the boiler.

He walked over. "Yeah."

"You have to do something for me, okay?"

"Sure." Reggie furrowed his brow. "What is it?"

Emerson bit her lip. "You can't die. You have to promise."

"I'll do my best." Reggie scratched his neck.

"No. It has to be a promise."

Reggie frowned. "Why?"

"If you die, I'll be stuck down here—alone." Emerson looked at the metal cover in the middle of the room.

Reggie pressed his lips together. "That's fair. Let's go."

TWENTY THREE
IT WANTS YOU

Reggie wrenched a pipe free from the derelict boiler, nearly falling backwards when it gave. Dollard and Emerson were by the door, eyes shut, trying to glean a path from the storage room to The Neon Heart. Dollard had his hands out like little radar dishes. Teal came over. Knife in hand.

"So, what did the kid want to say? Was she professing her undying love for you?"

Reggie smirked. "No. She wanted me to promise I wouldn't die and leave her stuck down here."

Teal chuckled. "That's fair."

"That's what I said."

"We're going to get through this, Reg." Teal rubbed his arm. "You take the lead, I'll cover the back wrangling those two as they keep alert to danger." She handed him the map she had taken off the wall.

"Just don't let me get too far ahead."

Teal raised an eyebrow. "I'm not too worried. You're the one with all those bites." She nudged him. "Time to go."

"Yeah." Reggie heaved the pipe over his shoulder and went to the door. "Anything?"

Dollard didn't open his eyes. "Hard to pinpoint. That thing is so slippery."

"We've got to move."

"It's as clear as it's going to get." Dollard sighed and let his arms drop.

"Love the optimism." Reggie stopped him from turning away. "Thank you. Things would be a lot worse off without you."

Dollard shook off Reggie's hand. "Yeah."

"Okay. You two stick between Teal and me. I'll be in the lead and she'll be watching our back. She'll also keep an eye on you, so do your best to keep an, uh, mental eye, on things. With no real weapons, we have to avoid running into anything the best we can and evade when we do."

"It's not easy." Emerson said.

"I know. We're all just going to do our best." Reggie opened the door. "Here we go."

The hallway was dark. The walls were made from bare cinder block with excessive gobs of mortar separating the seams. They were marked and stained, but Reggie couldn't tell from what. The only light he could see was spilling from the maintenance room behind them. He closed his eyes and switched the contacts he wore to night mode. When he looked again, everything was bathed in a yellow sheen. Details were washed out, but he could see the hallway more clearly.

It was wide, which made the ceiling feel lower than it was. The floor was mostly covered in debris and some kind of thin vines that branched out and snaked up the walls and ceiling. A track ran down the middle of the floor.

Teal was only a couple metres behind him, but Reggie used the comm to talk to her.

"What do you make of the tracks?"

"Some kind of cart or small rail car. I'm less concerned with that than those vines."

"Yeah?"

"What kind of vines grow in complete darkness?"

"Okay." Reggie nodded to himself.

"The bad kind."

"Got it."

"The bad kind of vines grow in darkness."

Reggie smirked. "Yes, Teal. I've got it." He held the pipe in both hands, across his body, and scanned back and forth as he jogged forward.

The tunnel forked into three directions. Each one the same shape and size. The tracks split with a complicated switching mechanism connecting them. The vines seemed to split along with the track, heading in, or coming from all three routes. A big light, like a squat cylinder coming down from the ceiling above the junction, was shattered. Scanning it with the contacts, Reggie couldn't detect any power running through the exposed wires.

He stopped and took out the map. Turning it to try and orient himself, he looked back at Dollard. "Any guesses?"

"Keep left." The Esper was breathing heavily.

Reggie stuffed the map in his pocket and got back to the jogging pace and led them down the left passage. The vines seemed to be thicker, but it was difficult to tell.

The tunnel continued to curve left and slope upwards. They passed a hallway running perpendicular that Reggie thought he could squeeze into, if he had to. It seemed to head to one of the tracks that had split off back at the junction.

"Keep going," Dollard said.

As they moved forward, Reggie managed to catch something scrawled on the wall. The words were mostly covered in vegetation, but large enough to still be seen.

"Anyone make that out? Your implants are better than my contact lenses in the dark."

"It wants you," Emerson said. "I think I can feel

it."

"That's just your imagination," said Dollard.

Reggie glanced behind him. "Just keep trying to sense—whatever is in these tunnels."

Dollard grabbed the back of Reggie's jacket, stopping him. "Wait."

Reggie stopped. "What?" he whispered.

"There." Dollard pointed over Reggie's shoulder.

Turning slowly, Reggie spotted a pale figure ahead of them. It was not much larger than a child and crouched next to the wall. "Where the hell did that come from?"

It turned its face towards them and Reggie saw huge dark circles where its eyes should be. In the night vision, he couldn't tell if they were huge eyes, or if the thing didn't have any at all. It was smaller than a scavenger, but seemed similarly mutated.

"That's not good," Teal said over the comm.

"You two picking anything up?" Reggie gripped his pipe tighter.

"It's scared," said Emerson. She sounded like she was trying to figure out a brain teaser. "Not of us, though. Not really."

"So it's not the thing we're trying to avoid?"

Dollard was still grabbing onto Reggie's jacket. "No, but…"

"Yeah?"

"It feels the same."

"What does that mean?"

The figure darted in the opposite direction, running like an ape, using its arms to help propel it forward.

"Did we scare it away?" Reggie asked.

Dollard and Emerson shrugged.

"Okay. Creepy. We keep going forward, I guess, watching for more of those, off-putting mutant child things." Reggie started to jog again, but slower than before. He felt the tug of Dollard on his jacket and looked back. The man realized he still held it and let go.

The tunnel leveled out and connected with a large round room. In the middle was a section of track on a turntable. From the center, tracks led in six directions to six identical tunnels.

Reggie stopped before entering the room. "Big open space. Perfect place for an ambush."

"Especially if that thing was bait," Teal said.

"Guys?" Reggie glanced at Dollard and Emerson then went back to surveying the round room.

"Hard to tell." Dollard had his hand out.

"It's stronger, the malevolence. I can't pinpoint it." Emerson had her eyes shut.

In the night vision, they looked pallid and tired. Reggie scratched his head. "Any sense on what way we should go?"

"Too many choices. It's all a jumble." Dollard lowered his arm. "I do feel more of those smaller things, though. Scattered. Every direction."

Teal leaned on Reggie's shoulder. "What does the map say?"

Reggie took out the scrap of paper. "From what I can tell, this junction isn't on it."

"We went up, so any of these tunnels go back down?"

Emerson pointed straight across the room. "That one does."

Reggie looked at Teal and shrugged. "Keep your eyes peeled."

He gripped the pipe and gingerly stepped into the room as if he were about to set off a snare with each footfall. They made it to the turntable and heard movement coming from their right. Reggie stopped, the line of people behind him bumping into each other. He turned to the where the sound had come from and peered into the darkness, willing the night vision to let him see farther. Behind them something scuttled, kicking up debris. He spun and caught sight of one of the creatures, possibly the same one they'd seen earlier. It sped into the tunnel. Another one dropped from above and joined it.

Emerson let out a whimper.

Dollard pulled her into an embrace. "It's here. It wants us."

Reggie turned back and saw two more pale, hunched figures emerging from the dark passageway. They seemed to be frantically running, galloping on their legs and arms. Before they made it to the room, something reached out and grabbed them both with one big pseudopod-like hand. The screeches the mutants made were cut short, but echoed in the circular room.

Reggie reached behind him and pushed Teal in the direction the smaller figures had been going. "Run, run, run, run."

She herded the Espers with her and Reggie backpedaled after them. In his night vision, he caught a glimpse of the creature as it emerged from the shadows. It seemed to fill the tunnel, pouring out of it like liquid. Limbs of varying sizes reached, pulled, and pushed it forward. Before he turned to run, he saw the faces. Hundreds of faces with hollow eyes like the small figures, mashed together into a single entity.

TWENTY FOUR
IT TRUNDLES

Reggie ran as quickly as he could. His legs felt sluggish and the cuts and bites from the insects burned. Ahead, he spotted Teal pushing Dollard and Emerson in front of her. The tunnel angled slightly downward and turned left. The huge, viscous creature flowed after them. Arm-like limbs reached out for them from its front as protrusions on all sides grabbed at the tunnel and propelled it forward. The decline seemed to aid its pursuit as it rolled forward, the limbs and faces receding into the mass and reappearing in the same position over and over again.

It gained on Reggie. He gritted his teeth and pushed himself through the pain. His injuries were shoved to the back of his mind as fear and adrenaline urged him to run harder. The tunnel leveled out, slowing his mad downhill dash. He hoped it would slow the thing down too. Concentrating on running, he didn't look back. He was gaining on Teal and the Espers, but felt his lungs burn from the effort and knew none of them could keep up the sprint for long.

As he caught up with the others, he threw the pipe behind him. He watched the mass of the creature absorb it without slowing down. Grabbing Dollard by the shoulders, he pushed the Esper forward, leaving Emerson to Teal.

"Can't… keep… this… up." Teal huffed, breathing heavily.

Reggie nodded. The coagulated thing was close, but without the help from gravity, they were staying just ahead of it.

Dollard pumped his arms, his coat flapping behind him. His foot caught the track, and he fell, tumbling. Reggie grabbed him by the jacket and pulled him up.

"Keep going." He half carried Dollard as the man got his feet back under him. A proboscis from the mass reached out in the form of a hand, and nearly grabbed Dollard. Reggie pulled until the Esper was in front of him. Just ahead, he saw Teal. She was stopped and waving at a spot in the wall.

They reached her and Reggie saw one of the small junction tunnels they had passed earlier. She ducked inside and Reggie pushed Dollard into the opening. He crouched and scrambled in after them as the creature reached for him. He could feel it at his back and scrambled forward, using his arms to help pull him through the small space like the creature had in the large tunnels.

Catching up with Dollard again, he looked back. The mass was stretching towards him with a cluster of arms filling the corridor. The hands grasped at the air behind Reggie and rebounded backwards, as if the creature couldn't squeeze itself any farther into the small space.

Reggie collapsed in the passageway and let out a weak laugh. "I think we got away."

"What?" Teal squeezed herself past Dollard.

"It can't fit." Reggie rubbed his eyes and leaned against the wall. His legs ached and the wounds burned as sweat leaked through the makeshift bandages.

Teal searched his jacket, which was nearly black in the dark tunnel, and took out the map. "Let me see if I can figure out where we are. You are useless with this thing."

The reaching arms receded back into the mass. Faces appeared on it, looking into the passageway. It let out a screech, like the smaller figures had, but in a chorus of hundreds. Reggie covered his ears and winced. It lumbered away.

"Did it actually just give up?" he asked to no one.

"I doubt it." Teal focused on the map, turning it

in her hands.

Dollard clutched his side and shook his head. "No. Still…"

"It's still after us," Emerson said. "It's driven to add us into its mass." She pulled her hair back and sighed.

Reggie got into a crouch. "We may be safe from that thing, for now, but if it can't get into these side tunnels, something else is going to be lurking in here."

"Yeah. I think I've got it." Teal held the map against the wall. She pointed at a spot in the middle of a cluster of squiggly lines. "I think it's our scale that's messed up. If we're here, this line here is where we crossed that turntable." She lowered the map and turned to face the far end of the tunnel they were in. "That means if we go that way and stick to these smaller passages, we should be going almost straight towards the elevator."

She smiled. "And, you are welcome."

Reggie shifted his weight. "Thank you. Care to lead the way?"

"I'd be delighted." Teal squeezed back past Dollard and Emerson. "Follow me, I've got the map."

They trudged towards the end of the tunnel and stopped at the point where they guessed the creature couldn't reach them. Teal put up her hand and crept forward silently. She hugged the wall and peeked into the larger passageway.

Reggie heard her whisper over the comm.

"Looks clear. I can see the next access tunnel." Without looking back, she waved them forward.

When they were gathered at the mouth of the passage she darted across the open space and slid down the wall to the small opening. When the coast was clear, she waved them to her again. Reggie stuck to the back, scanning for the creature or anything else that may be following them. He felt helpless without the pipe, but kept his guard up.

They slipped into the other tunnel and repeated the same process. At the end of the fourth access tunnel, they saw the first light since the maintenance closet. Teal checked the map.

"This is it. The light at the end of the tunnel and the end of this train system, or whatever it is. From here it seems to be all part of that big complex we saw on the surface. It's laid out almost like a smaller version of city streets. We just have to cross some big room."

Reggie found the spot on the map she was holding. It was marked like the location of The Neon Heart, but instead of a cartoon, someone had drawn a winged figure with its arms raised. He checked his comm-band. There was just over two hours left on the clock.

"Time for Teal and me to do our thing," he said.

"If you sense anything, let us know over the comm, but other than that, keep your heads down and stay hidden the best you can. I don't think the regular Neon Heart security will be much trouble, but I have no idea what to expect from the Consortium operatives."

Emerson and Dollard nodded.

Dollard wiped his brow. "I wanted to, uh. That is. Thank you for helping me back there."

Reggie grinned. "We wouldn't have gotten this far without you."

Dollard looked away and cleared his throat. "Yes—well. Back to it."

Joining Teal at the opening, Reggie took a deep breath.

"Are you ready?" Teal asked.

"You're the one with the knife."

"I know it's kind of weird, but I'm a little excited to be going up against some regular old operatives. Ya know?"

Reggie furrowed his brow. "There are going to be lot of them, Teal."

"I know, but it's just people. We've handled people before."

"I guess." Reggie looked at his empty hands.

Teal winked at him. "Let's go have some fun."

TWENTY FIVE
JUST PEOPLE

Reggie leaned around Teal and peered into the open space. The room was mostly dark. The light they had seen from the tunnel came from an exit on the far wall. It was dim but he had to squint until his lenses adjusted to it. The room was cavernous with a ceiling arching into shadows. He made out a row of carved pillars, some of them broken and crumbled, and could just see more at the edge of the light—the night vision struggling with the contrast. In between them were some smashed benches and rubble. There was what looked like a big fountain right in the center, on a dais.

Strewn about the room were statues, most of them fallen or pushed over and in pieces. The one in the best condition was like the drawing on the map. A winged figure with arms raised, though one of the wings was clipped on the end.

Reggie focused on the source of light. Flanking the opening in the wall were floodlights attached to stands. Beyond that, he could see a lit hallway and the faint outlines of people.

Teal nudged him and pointed to the shapes. "I count five."

He leaned towards them. "I only see four."

"One is sitting."

"Damn. Yep, there he is."

"What's the plan?"

Reggie scratched his chin. "We have to assume at least one of them has an implant."

Teal sneered. "Maybe some back-alley hack job."

Reggie glared at her.

"Right. Continue."

"Even if we avoid the light, they may be able to see us. We have to stay low, move slowly, and hope they don't spot us."

"Inspired." Teal raised an eyebrow.

"You have something better?"

"No. Let's go." Teal dropped to the floor and crawled to the wreckage of a fallen pillar. She slipped behind it and held her position.

Reggie clenched his fist and got to his belly. Every wound on his chest and legs twinged with pain. Keeping as low as possible, he moved from shadow to shadow. He stuck closer to the wall than Teal, working his way towards the guards.

"In position," Teal whispered over the comm.

"Dang, did you run?"

"I'm just not a slow old man."

"I'm an injured old man." Reggie stifled a grunt as he pulled himself over the remains of a broken bench. "I'm going to be a minute still."

"Got it. Holding."

Reggie crawled behind the base of the mostly intact statue and sat up. He leaned against the plinth and checked his injuries. Blood leaked through his torn pants from some of the deeper gashes. Feeling around on the ground, he grabbed a fragment of a stone with a jagged edge and got into a crouch.

"Okay," he said. "I'm as ready as I'll ever—"

Before Reggie could give the signal, the back wall crashed inward with a discordant boom that bounded around the room and raced into the shadows above. Bright light shone in, silhouetting the gelatinous blob that quivered as it screamed in chorus.

"What the hell?" Teal said over the comm.

The guards opened fire. They yelled conflicting orders, panicked by the creature.

Reggie managed to pick out someone saying 'it's here' over and over again.

"Change of plans." Reggie sprinted for the tunnel. "I'm getting Dollard and Emerson. We rush that patrol while they're occupied and get the hell out of here."

"Uh-huh. I'll watch your back."

Reggie looked over his shoulder. He saw the lithe shape of Teal emerge from her hiding space. She had managed to get within ten feet of the guards. In a flash, she cut one down, took his gun, and darted into another shadow.

"Don't kill them all, they're holding that thing back."

The creature undulated into the room, letting more light fill the space. Reggie glimpsed ornate fixtures on the walls and an altar, just before it was enveloped by the creature. It leaked some kind of dark fluid where it was shot, and moved much more slowly than it had in the tunnels.

He got to the Espers and pulled them to the nearest pillar. A few stray bullets hit the stone around them, but most of the focus was on the steadily advancing monster. It reached out several proboscises, one towards Reggie, the rest focused on the guards.

Reggie peeked around the corner of the pillar. The creature's vain grasp drew the attention of the patrol. Grabbing Emerson and Dollard's coats, he led them to a fallen statue and pulled them to the ground.

"What do you want me to do here, Reg?" Teal asked.

"Get ready to make a hole for us. I want to leave them to deal with each other and get to the Heart as quickly as possible."

"On it."

Reggie led the Espers down the wall, to the pillar nearest to the guards. "Now."

Teal popped out of cover on the opposite side and fired over the heads of The Neon Heart's security. They ducked and one of them changed his focus to the new threat. Reggie kept Emerson and Dollard moving, pushing them behind the distracted security and into the hallway. He let the Espers get ahead and dove onto one of the guards, stripping the man of his gun. Rolling back to his feet, Reggie let off a shot next to the man shooting at Teal. The recoil kicked his shoulder back like a mule, but he made an opening for her.

The guards got back up and two of them chose Reggie and his squad as a bigger threat than the creature from the tunnels. A few bullets hit the walls behind them as they ran away from the chaos.

"Don't worry about them," another guard screamed. "Stop that thing from getting through the perimeter."

Reggie glanced back and saw the man yell into a makeshift comm-band, presumably giving details of the event to the other patrols or to the Heart itself, then continue to shoot at the monster.

Joining Teal and the others, Reggie checked the rifle he'd taken from the guard. It was well-worn with a lever-action and a long barrel. He removed the clip. It was small, but the cartridges were big. He didn't have many shots, but the ones he had would put a hole through an armored soldier, if the recoil didn't tear his arm off. Teal had a fully-automatic machine gun, much smaller, but with a long clip curving at the end.

Dollard was stopped next to Emerson, a few metres farther down the hall. The girl was shaking and he was trying to calm her down. He looked at Reggie and shook his head.

"She's overwhelmed. With her own stress and all the people she's reading."

Reggie crouched next to Emerson. "Hey. I know this sucks, but we need to move. Don't worry about anything but putting one foot in front of the other and staying with either Teal or me. It's a sprint to the finish, okay."

Emerson wiped her eyes and nodded.

"We're going to get up now, okay?" Reggie helped her stand and glanced at Dollard.

The Esper took her by the arm. "More are on the way. Not just these local goons. Operatives."

Reggie half-smiled. "Of course. Let's go."

With Teal covering their back, he led them down the corridor at a jog. The floors were covered in linoleum tiles with grooves and pits from years of people walking a set route. Old paint peeled and flecked off the walls, leaving chips gathered where the floor and walls met. Square fixtures on the ceiling cast weak blue-tinted light. It felt like the basement of a large building.

"This has got to be that complex where we saw the elevator." Teal pulled out the map as they ran.

"What was this place?" Dollard asked.

Reggie shrugged, looking down the hallway. "Some company that failed long ago, or was amalgamated into a bigger conglomerate that eventually became the Corporations. All that matters is that this is where we can find the Heart."

Teal tapped the map. "The Heart is close, but there is a large grid of corridors between it and us and it's filled with more guards and Consortium operatives."

Reggie glanced back at her. "Still having fun?"

THE NEON HEART

TWENTY SIX
CONSORTIUM
OPERATIVES

Reggie held the rifle ready as they approached the first corner. Hesitating, he motioned for Dollard and Emerson to wait and peered around the wall. A squad of five operatives in black and red outfits was running towards them. One of them spotted him and raised a compact-blaster. Reggie jumped back as a section of the wall was vaporized.

"Contact." Taking a sharp breath, he rolled into the open, stopping with his rifle shouldered. He fired, catching the blaster-wielder in the chest. Reggie used the massive recoil to stumble backwards and get to his feet. The operative he'd shot was splayed on the floor, most of his middle missing. He dove back out of the corridor as Teal slipped under him.

She stuck tight to the corner, looking down the sight of her machine gun. The weapon sounded like a mad woodpecker as she found her target, fired, then found the next one.

"Two down." Teal backed away from the wall and checked her ammunition. "Draw them in?"

"If they're smart, they'll just wait for backup."

Dollard tapped Reggie on the shoulder. "They seem to be more reckless than that."

Reggie nodded. "On three."

Teal slapped the bottom of her magazine, locking it into place. "Roger." She winked.

Reggie counted down and stepped out. He saw one of the remaining operatives take aim but shot him first.

Before the last agent could retaliate, Teal took him down. Reggie slung the rifle over his shoulder and ran to the bodies. He took a handgun from one of them and extra ammunition. The others came over and Reggie held up a second pistol to Dollard.

"I suppose that's the pertinent decision." The Esper took the gun, holding it like he was out of practice.

"Emerson?" Reggie looked up at the girl.

She pressed her lips together and tensed up.

"Don't worry about it. Stick with Teal."

Teal put an arm around her and squeezed. "Watch my back." She dropped the machine gun and grabbed the blaster and a more modern assault rifle with a basic tracking screen. "That's more like it."

"Incoming." Dollard held his pistol out towards

the hallway the Consortium operatives had come down.

"How many?" Reggie rummaged through the pockets of the dead agents.

"Lots. A dozen or so."

"A welcoming party," Teal said.

Reggie stood. "Should we say hello?"

Taking the lead again, he ran ahead of the group. He spotted a junction where another hallway intersected and posted up at the corner. Checking each direction for approaching agents, he reached out to Teal. "Map."

"What's the magic word?" Teal handed the paper over to him without waiting for the answer.

"Thanks." Reggie spun on the spot, orienting the map to his surroundings.

"What do you have?" Teal asked.

"If that temple is south, we're going northwest." He stuffed the map into his pocket. "Straight or left?"

"They're coming from the west," Dollard said.

"Left it is." Reggie took another peek before he ran down the intersecting hallway. There were junctions every fifteen metres. Reggie paused at each one to check for operatives or guards and kept running forward.

He reached a wall and took a right turn, heading north. The pattern continued, with hallways branching off east at regular intervals. He slowed down and waited for the others to catch up and looked back at Dollard. "Where are these operatives we're supposed to run into?"

Dollard shrugged, breathing heavily.

"Maybe we slipped past them?" Teal said.

"They're close." Emerson looked up. Her eyes went wide and she snapped her head to the right, facing the next hallway.

Reggie sprinted past the opening, catching sight of the operatives charging towards them, and slid to a stop at the following junction. He tucked against the corner and waited for the first soldier to reach the opening he'd past. Three popped into the corridor aiming for him. They were dressed in the same black and red Consortium outfit. Reggie shot one in the head, hitting the operative's facemask. The soldier fell backwards, but slipped back into the adjoining hallway. The other two were hit from behind by Teal's confiscated blaster. What was left of them smoldered on the floor.

Reggie ran east to the next junction. He turned south to backtrack and catch the operatives in a crossfire, but they must have been thinking the same thing, because he ran into two Consortium agents coming around the corner. Reggie shot, hitting the first one in the chest. He kept running and got close enough to the second to knock the operative's gun back and smash his pistol into her facemask. She staggered back as the one he had shot got to his feet.

The man wheezed, the impact of the bullet on his body armor knocking the wind out of him. Reggie kicked him into the wall, winced from opening a bunch of his fresh wounds, and stuck the tip of his pistol under the man's visor. He shot without looking, turning to face the second soldier.

The woman held her machine pistol out, but her arm wavered. Reggie feigned left, drawing her aim wide, and stepped in on the right. He grabbed her arm and snapped it down onto his shoulder. She dropped her gun. As it clattered to the ground, Reggie shot her in her exposed neck and let her body drop.

He scooped up the machine pistol and moved to the corner—behind the other operatives. A group of them were huddled against the far wall, in a firefight with Teal and Dollard. Four others were heading towards Reggie. They stopped when they saw him and opened fire. Reggie let loose with the machine pistol, shooting past them to the soldiers engaged with Teal. He saw two of them drop, joining other bodies on the linoleum floor. Their attention was drawn to him, giving Teal the opportunity to either return fire unhindered, or run. Another operative fell, giving Reggie his answer.

Backing away from the hall, he stuck the machine pistol in his belt along with the handgun. He swung the rifle off his back and dropped to a knee. The first agent came around the corner at a sprint, likely meaning to catch him off guard. Reggie fired, sending the soldier into the air. The body dropped with a thud, a crater in its torso. Reggie cocked the lever to slip another cartridge into place. A smaller operative slipped in the blood spilling out from her fallen comrade and right into Reggie's line of sight. He fired again, catching her as she tried to turn and run. Her body spun and crumpled on top of the first.

Reggie cocked the lever again, but didn't hear the familiar click of a bullet entering the chamber. He dropped the big rifle with a thud that matched the sound the dead operatives had made and pulled his pistol. Standing, he sprinted through the junction, jumping over the bodies.

The operatives flinched at seeing him, giving him enough time to get clear before they could target him. He turned left at the next hallway, coming behind his own group. Dollard was crouched at the far corner, aiming towards him. The Esper fired, but put his hands up when he noticed it was Reggie.

The bullet hit the wall close enough to make Reggie stumble. He put his arms out to stop from smashing his face into the floor and scrambled to his feet.

"Sorry." Dollard still had his hands up.

"We're good. Keep watching our back." Reggie patted the Esper's shoulder.

Teal had dropped the blaster and was smacking the assault rifle with the palm of her hand. "Thing jammed on me. I was better off with that old piece of crap."

"Got you a present." Reggie held out the machine pistol.

Teal took it with a grin. "You're a peach." She let the rifle drop and swung around the corner, spraying the hallway with bullets.

"Time to go. We can't get pinned down. They'll just keep getting reinforcements." Reggie glanced down the hallway Dollard was covering.

"I've got an idea for that." Teal pulled back, still smiling.

"Yeah?"

"One of those Consortium idiots had a plasma thrower. If I can get to it, I can set it to overload."

Reggie scrunched up his face. "Even if you can get to it, and prime it, how are we supposed to get away if they can just pin us down here?"

"I'd better hurry, then." Teal winked and dashed around the corner.

THE NEON HEART

TWENTY SEVEN
SURFACE OF
THE SUN

"Watch out!" Dollard reached back and pulled on Reggie's jacket.

Turning to see what Dollard wanted, Reggie dropped to the floor. A blaster bolt cooked the air where he had been standing and exploded against the back wall.

Dollard fired, pushing the operative back into cover. Reggie got to his feet and sprinted for the corner. "Watch out for Teal," he yelled over his shoulder.

The operative darted back out, blaster in hand. Reggie dove under the blast again as it splashed against the floor behind him, singeing his pants and shoes. Rolling with his dive, Reggie found his footing and lunged, tackling the agent. He fought over the blaster, using gravity to help force the man's arm to the ground. The operative rocked forward, bashing

Reggie in the face with his helmeted head.

Reggie reeled back, giving the man leverage to flip him onto his back and gain the upper hand. The operative forced the blaster at Reggie. With blood flowing from his nose and his eyes watering, Reggie gritted his teeth, fighting the man.

As the soldier twisted his grip, forcing Reggie to let go of the blaster, he was tackled again.

Dollard rolled with the operative, ending up in the same position Reggie had been in, but with the blaster on the floor out of reach. Reggie grabbed it and kicked the operative in the helmet. As the man fell backwards, Reggie shot him, melting the helmet and everything underneath it.

He helped Dollard to his feet. "Teal?"

Dollard held his side and winced.

Reggie turned to face another direction, but had to reorient himself. He spotted Emerson staring at them and ran towards her. Teal sprang around the corner, grabbed Emerson by the oversized jacket, and waved them away.

"Run!" She pulled the girl behind her and waved again.

Reggie turned back to Dollard and prodded the Esper into motion. "Go, go, go!"

Teal sped past them, Emerson in tow. "Move!"

Reggie ran after her, keeping Dollard in front of him. They passed hallway after hallway in the grid-like basement. Teal took a left, heading north, and they followed. They sprinted through another junction and Reggie saw more operatives sweeping the corridors, searching for them. One of the soldiers spotted them and yelled for them to stop. Letting off some un-aimed shots, Reggie kept running. He prodded Dollard to keep the pace up.

"Almost there!"

Dollard held his side and waved his hand in Reggie's face. "No... Turn... Coming towards us..."

Reggie nodded and yelled to Teal over the comm. "Dollard says there's a group ahead of us."

Teal didn't answer, but Reggie saw her take the next left. He followed in time to see her change direction again, keeping them heading north.

"Almost out of this section," Teal said.

Reggie was about to reply, but a loud boom, accompanied by an unnatural whine, shook the hallways around them. Dollard lost his footing as the floor cracked under their feet.

"All or nothing." Reggie helped steady Dollard. They sprinted forward, the air around them rumbling and growing hot. Cracks in the floor and walls caused by the initial explosion spread faster than they could run, foreshadowing the wave of fire and plasma that was racing through the basement, vaporizing everything in its way.

Reggie spotted Teal up ahead. She made it to a

hallway that looked different from the rest. It only had the one entrance as far as he could see. He heard screaming behind them, piercing the rumbling sound, and risked a glance over his shoulder. He could see the light from the approaching plasma, red, orange, and yellow. It was the brightest thing he'd seen since going underground, and the blast was still out of view.

"Come on!" Teal had one foot in the new tunnel and looked like a rabbit about to bolt. She grabbed Dollard as they approached and helped Reggie half carry the Esper down the curving corridor.

Reggie breathed heavily and felt his cuts burning again. "How far—"

"—not sure, but the plasma thrower was half full, so I don't want to risk coming up short."

They caught up to Emerson who was limping. Reggie scooped her up and tossed her over his shoulder, leaving Dollard to Teal. "We can't get much farther."

The rumble continued to chase them heating up the cool basement. The hallway straightened out and connected with a larger, rectangular hall that looked like an old lobby for the building. On the far end of the room, Reggie saw another security post, four guards who looked like Wall residents were standing around a berm made from dirt and rubble.

They kept running towards the guards who

seemed shocked to see them. Reggie yelled for them to get down, feeling the heat grow behind him. One of the guards raised his weapon and Teal cut him down with the machine pistol.

"I said get down!" Reggie pulled his own pistol, still carrying Emerson. Two of the guards dropped their weapons and held up their hands, the other took aim. He and Teal shot them and dove over the berm. Reggie grabbed the legs of one of the remaining guards and pulled him down, but the other just looked down at them.

They could feel the floor rumbling, but they were still ahead of the plasma.

"What's going on?" The guard who Reggie had pulled down still had his hands up.

"We were running away from a plasma explosion, but we may have gotten out of its range." Reggie pushed the man's hands down.

"Plasma?" The still standing guard asked as the rumble swept into the room, throwing heat and light over everything like a solar flare.

Reggie shut his eyes and let the heat pass over them. The sound of the plasma cutting through the air was like standing in front of a ship's horn.

It went on for several minutes. The heat and pressure made it feel like they were being cooked. Then it stopped.

Reggie blinked. Even with his eyes closed and

his head to the ground, he saw spots. His exposed skin was tender and pink. The walls were splashed with swaths of black and the linoleum floor was cured and charred. The scorched body of the standing guard crumpled, a wet splat accompanying the thud.

Grimacing, Reggie turned away from the body and sat up. "How is everyone?"

"Dollard?" Teal said. "Reggie, something's wrong with Dollard."

TWENTY EIGHT
THE HEART

Reggie crawled over to Dollard. The Esper was on his back, holding his side. Teal had his head in her lap.

"Hey. What's wrong?" Reggie opened the man's long jacket and pulled his hand away. Blood leaked from a bullet wound. Closing his eyes, Reggie clenched his jaw and rode out a wave of anger. "When did this happen?"

Dollard coughed. "In the temple. Between that thing and those guards."

"Why didn't you say anything?" Teal asked, stroking his hair.

"You know me. Team player."

Reggie went to touch the wound and hesitated. "That's a lot of blood loss. We need to stop the bleeding and get you out of here."

Standing, Reggie turned on the guard who had

surrendered. "Where's the Heart?"

He was still crouched behind the barrier.

Reggie reached down and grabbed the man, hauling him to his feet. "The Neon Heart! Where is it?"

"I—I can't." The man looked away.

Reggie shoved him into the nearest wall. He screamed, trying to push away from the blackened surface.

"I'm not screwing around. You are going to show me where it is or I'm going to make you pay for that man's pain." Reggie gestured to Dollard with a nod.

"Okay, okay! I'll take you there. It's not far."

Reggie spun the man to face the hallway. "Teal. You want to take this? I'll carry Dollard."

"Um." Teal wiped her face. "He's gone." Shuffling back, Teal gently lowered Dollard's head to the floor. She stood, gesturing for Emerson to do the same. "Let's go."

Reggie balled up his fist then relaxed it with a sigh. "Okay. Time to get this over with."

A low rhythmic sound emanated from the way they'd come. Reggie stopped to look behind him. The noise grew and was joined by yells, faint in the distance.

"You think some of those operatives made it through that blast?"

"I don't want to wait around to find out," Teal said.

Reggie waved at the hallway in front of the guard. "Lead the way."

The man hesitated. Reggie shoved him. "If you think those Consortium soldiers are going to save you, I can tell you now that I'll shoot you before they get me. Okay?"

The guard looked back at Reggie, wide-eyed.

"Yeah. Move it."

The man started to walk. Reggie prodded him into a run, and they left the scorched lobby behind them. He led then past a series of identical corridors and down one of them, stopping at the end.

The door to The Neon Heart was painted in pink and blue. Made of steel, there were rivets around the outer edge and across the middle. Coming across it at random, or searching every offshoot of the main hallway for it would have taken them hours.

Reggie rapped on the metal door with his gun.

"Maybe there's a secret knock or something?" Teal said.

"Maybe," Reggie said. He banged again and a slit opened in the middle of the door. Before the person behind it could close it, Reggie stuck the barrel of his pistol into the slot.

"Open up."

He could only see the person's eyes. They looked at the gun, then to the guard that Teal had up against the back wall. He heard a series of clicks and pushed the door open, moving his gun to cover the interior of The Neon Heart.

Teal went in first, leading the guard. Emerson followed. Reggie took a last look in the hallway before going in, closing the door behind him. He checked the locks. Several mismatched deadbolts were drilled into the metal door. On either side was a bracket that seemed like they could hold a bar to prevent the door from swinging inward. Reggie searched on either side and found a metal pipe that looked like it fit in the slots. He put it in place and let his shoulders drop.

"That will only buy us a few minutes. Those operatives are not far behind." He turned to face the rest of the bar.

The space was illuminated with blue and pink lights, nearly the same colour as the door. It looked as if the original founders of the Heart broke through the walls of the room to expand into the adjacent ones to make more space. Parts of the broken walls were still there, making uneven openings with the paths of least resistance marked by years of wear. In the main room, a wooden counter ran along one wall. Behind it, makeshift shelves covered in dusty bottles surrounded a dirty mirror.

An old man stood behind the bar. His beard glowed under the neon, looking like it was a light source itself. He snorted when Reggie looked at him, and spat on the floor. The intrusion didn't seem to bother him in the slightest.

Through the wall on the opposite side, Reggie could see tables with glasses and bottle still set on them. Either people cleared out another way when he, Teal and Emerson forced their way in, or the bartender didn't bother to clear the tables. Reggie poked his head farther into the room and saw a couple of folks sitting at a high table, still drinking.

There was a set of double doors in the back room, added to the wall with more care than the broken opening he was peering through. Reggie ignored it and went back to the main space.

Teal continued to cover the guard. She had him and the doorman in the corner between the partially opened wall where Reggie stood and the more demolished one at the back of the room.

A large, square cage made of mismatched pieces of fence and chicken wire extended from the middle of the back room up through the ceiling. He saw the elevator car behind a closed scissor gate and a man sitting next to an old terminal beside it. Boxes were piled into the corners and against the walls. Standing tables were crammed into the remaining open space. The whole place looked like any backwater bar that

Reggie had seen on any number of settlements—more dirty and cobbled together than most, but familiar.

Reggie went to the bar. He rubbed his chin. "I'm here to see the device."

The bartender snorted again. "Don't know what you mean."

Sighing, Reggie glanced back at Teal and frowned. "Look. We both know what this is about. I am in no mood. As I told that guy back there, the one with my friend's gun in his face, I'll kill everyone in the room before the Consortium gets through that door. You may as well give up and live."

"Don't have anything to do with that. I'm just the bartender."

A bang at the door drew Reggie's attention. "Okay. Well that's them."

"We know you're in there. Give up now and we'll let you live," A muffled voice yelled from behind the thick metal.

"That's what I said." Reggie looked back at Teal again.

"Pretty close, yeah."

Emerson cleared her throat. "Someone's trying to read us."

"Behind the door?" Reggie asked.

"And back there." She pointed to the wall in the elevator room. "Somewhere."

"Okay. And you've got it covered?"

She nodded.

"Good. Thank you." Reggie backed away from the bar. "Now we're getting somewhere."

The banging at the door continued, ramping up to slams. The door shook and the pipe creaked.

"Not a lot of time," Teal said.

Reggie scratched his chin again. "Forward it is." He went over to the pile of boxes in the back room and pulled them away. Bottles smashed against the floor, spilling the acrid liquid inside. He spotted a door behind the stack and cleared the way.

"Aha. There it is." He tried the handle, but it was locked. Stepping back, he kicked the door open, splintering the frame. "Knock, knock."

THE NEON HEART

TWENTY NINE
TIME TRAVEL
IS BULLSHIT

A wave of heat emanated from the doorway. The room was filled with thin smoke, making Reggie wrinkle his nose. He expected to see a fire, but the smoke was coming from a bank of computer racks that took up the back half of the space. A long metal table was against the wall to his left, filled with wires, computer parts, and tools. On the opposite wall, a man huddled behind a device that looked like a cross between a virtual reality harness and a medieval torture device. Components were strapped down to planks of weathered wood, connected by wires and scrap pieces of metal. The whole thing surrounded a simple plastic chair with a burn mark on the seat that looked like someone dropped a cigarette and never bothered to clean it up.

The man was wearing dirty coveralls. His face was covered in grease except for the mark around his eyes from the goggles he had resting on his head. Reggie couldn't tell how old the man was under the filth, but his scraggly hair was blond punctuated with streaks of grime.

"Get up." Reggie waved for the man to stand.

"You shouldn't b-be here. You we-we-weren't invited." The man tried to retreat behind the chair.

"I don't have time for this. Start this stupid thing up." Reggie snapped his fingers and pointed to the contraption.

"No."

Reggie sighed and pointed his gun. "That chair isn't going to stop this bullet."

"Y-you can't d-d-do this to me. I-I am a sc-scientist." The man stood, haltingly, like his speech.

"You're a pain in my ass and the indirect cause of the deaths of four of my squad members. So, think long and hard about how patient I'm being right now."

"The t-t-t-ime machine is m-m-my ticket out of this place." The man put his hands up and shuffled out from behind the contraption.

"I don't care. This entire sector is property of the Telbak Corporation. You should have gone to them." Reggie frowned. He felt a headache coming on.

"Th-They would have j-just t-t-taken it from me."

"Now I'm taking it from you."

"Y-y-you aren't T-Telbak." The man smiled. "I-I'll s-sell it to Amcoral. Full rights for a single share."

"I'm not here to buy this piece of crap. You have ten seconds to turn it on before I write off this whole contract and burn everything to the ground."

Teal came to the doorway, her machine pistol still aimed towards the bar. "We're running out of time. That door won't hold out much longer."

Emerson slipped into the room, past Teal.

Reggie clenched his teeth.

"Th-the C-C-C-Consortium. They'll deal with y-you." The man lowered his hands.

Reggie sneered, closing the distance to the inventor. He pushed the man into the plastic chair and pressed his pistol against the man's temple. "My patience is up. Five seconds."

"Wait." Emerson came up behind them and put her hand on Reggie's arm. "I can do this quicker."

Reggie stepped away. He took a deep breath.

Emerson pulled the hair away from her face and leaned over the man, staring into his eyes. She closed her own and slowly leaned in until their foreheads were almost touching.

Reggie looked at Teal. "Door?"

"Still standing. One of the brackets holding that pipe in place is looking pretty loose."

Turning back to Emerson, Reggie saw her

219

straighten.

"It's bullshit." Emerson backed away from the inventor. "It reads memories, creates a virtual simulation. Makes people think they've seen the past. And…" Emerson put her hand out the way Dollard had when he scanned something. "It rots your brain while it does it."

"Works for me. Time to go."

"On it." Teal went over to the man sitting at the elevator terminal. "Up."

The man stood and backed away.

Reggie pointed his pistol back at the inventor. "Since you seem to be the one in charge, I'll ask you. What can we expect at the top of the elevator?"

Emerson spoke first. "Most of the operatives we saw at the top were sent down here when we broke through their perimeter. They left a skeleton crew to guard it."

"That's the first good news we've had since we got here." Reggie took aim at the computer racks and fired until more smoke poured out of them. It turned black and curled away from the machines in twisting columns. He saw a flicker of light as a fire caught. It quickly spread across the computers.

"Teal?" Reggie left the room and covered the rest of the bar patrons. The guard who led them there kept his hands up.

"I think I got it. I can't lock them out once we're

on our way up, though."

"Can we destroy the terminal and still go up?"

"Maybe?" Teal dashed over to the scissor gate, looked up the shaft, and went back to the terminal "I think so."

"Let's do it."

The door to the Heart shook and Reggie heard a ping as one of the bolts holding the brackets to the wall broke.

"Get in." Teal pulled open the bottom hatch of the terminal as Reggie and Emerson got on the elevator. Reggie aimed his pistol at the door.

Teal pulled free a handful of wires. She twisted two of them together and the elevator shuttered. The cable at the top of the car was pulled taut and it started to rise. Teal jammed her knife into the thick bundle of wires that ran from the terminal up the shaft, and dove into the car. Reggie grabbed her arm and pulled her inside before they were lifted into the cage, cutting off the doorway.

"I hope that does it." Teal got to her feet and brushed herself off. "At least we're moving."

"Hopefully they don't have time to get reinforcements to the top before we get there." Reggie watched the pattern of the cage crawl by as they moved away from the bottom of the Wall towards the surface. He checked his comm-band. There was an hour and a half left on his countdown. "It's a little slow, isn't it?"

"Better than going back the way we came."

From below them, Reggie heard shouting. "Sounds like they got through the door."

"Moment of truth." Teal crossed her arms and leaned against the wall. "Any bets?"

Emerson put her hand to her temple. "I can feel their anger. Frustration."

"Can you sense a plan?" Reggie asked.

Emerson shook her head. "No. It's—Move!" Emerson shoved Reggie against the wall as bullets ripped through the floor.

"They're desperate!" Teal pulled the machine pistol from her belt and fired back down. "This is annoying."

"They're going to hit one of us eventually." Reggie waited for Teal to stop shooting and fired off a few rounds.

Wisps of smoke crept through the holes in the floor.

"Cover your mouths!" Reggie pulled his tattered shirt over his nose. "Maybe that fire will push them away from the shaft."

Teal put her arm over her face. "What's better, getting shot or choking to death?"

Reggie glared at her. "I hope we can get out of here before it gets too bad."

"Out of the frying pan, am I right?"

THIRTY

SURFACING

The trails of dense black smoke spewing out of the bullet holes and creeping in around the cage filled the shaft by the time they approached the surface. When the motion of the car slowed, Reggie squinted at the doors. His eyes stung and the shallow breaths he took burned in his mouth and chest. He hoped the Goliath transport that was waiting for him had a good medical bay.

He rubbed Emerson's back. The Esper coughed, struggling in the smoke.

Teal tapped him on the chest, getting his attention. She moved right up to his face and made a series of hand motions, briefly explaining a plan.

Reggie shook his head. He pointed to her and Emerson then the elevator.

Teal frowned under the shirt covering her face and the doors opened. The smoke building at the top of the shaft billowed out, spinning in a maelstrom as it met the cooler outside air.

Crouching low, Reggie ran through the cloud. He went straight for the far end of the courtyard and spotted the fence his group had hid behind earlier in the day.

The smoke trailed after him, dissipating around him as he ran. He changed his direction, anticipating incoming fire from behind, but the shot that just missed him came from above—from one of the buildings surrounding the courtyard. Stopping against the closest wall, he looked back at the elevator. He coughed and spat, feeling lightheaded.

Through the billowing cloud, he spotted dead Consortium operatives scattered on the ground.

Reggie called to Teal over the comm. "They were ambushed. Someone in the buildings. I'll draw their fire."

Pushing away a wave of dizziness, Reggie ran back towards the smoke, but cut to the left, running across the open courtyard. He heard the shots as they were fired, and the bullets hit the ground next to him, but the sounds echoed in the enclosed space, making it impossible for him to pinpoint their source.

He heard a spray of bullets fired from behind and changed direction, expecting to be shot in the back.

"Got one," Teal yelled. "There's another. North, three stories up. Middle window." She started to cough. "Kid says more on the way."

Reggie spun, sliding to a stop. He aimed at the place Teal said, a red brick building with brown water stains marring its facade. He spotted the glint of a scope in the window and fired. A body slumped forward, falling onto a fire escape. The sniper was in all red clothing with long red hair cascading through the grated floor.

"Shit, Teal?" Reggie scanned the courtyard, but his vision was foggy. He shook his head.

"Over here!" Teal was standing by the fence.

Reggie ran over and stumbled, slamming against the wood boards, making them shudder.

"You okay?" Teal helped steady him.

"Got the shakes." Reggie clenched his fists.

Teal wiped soot off of his cheek. Her own face was smeared with black. "You're crashing. Been running on adrenalin for too long. That smoke didn't help." She poked him in the chin. "Neither did that daring run out of the elevator."

"You can give me your criticism when we're on the shuttle." Reggie took a deep breath.

"I'm on point, watch Emerson." Teal scrambled over the fence. "Clear, send her over."

Reggie made a foothold with his hands. "You ready?"

Emerson nodded. "Yeah. Headache."

"Me too. It'll pass."

Emerson stepped on Reggie's hands and he lifted her onto the fence. When she was over, he scrambled up after her. On the other side, Teal was already checking around the next corner.

"So, the Red Gang attacked the Consortium?" Reggie moved next to Teal.

She shrugged. "I guess. Maybe they always planned to. Maybe things went sour? It's not so important right now."

Reggie nodded. "You remember the way?"

"You don't?" Teal smiled. Her teeth were vibrant white compared to her smudged face. "We need to hurry or they'll be all over us. We're also running out of time. I want to get paid for all this trouble and get my report in so the companies pay out to the families of our friends."

"Lead the way." Reggie checked his stolen pistol. He was running low on ammunition and guessed Teal had less than he did.

With Teal out front, they jogged from the alley to a long corridor, and through the main floor of an apartment complex. The lobby had been partitioned into rooms with plywood and plastic sheet walls, leaving a narrow path between them to the other side. They wound through more tunnels that twisted around the small spaces left between buildings. Reggie felt like he was back underground until they made it to an open walkway. Teal led them into another building and picked the lock on the door to a laundry room with a piece of wire she stripped from a broken panel on the wall. Washing machines stacked against the wall whirred and whined, but there was no one there.

"We're getting close, I think." Teal leaned on her knees. "I feel like we're moving faster than before, but I'm winded from that smoke."

"No detour to the market." Reggie raised an eyebrow. "Emerson. Any sign of the Reds?"

"They know we're above ground, but they don't know where we are. I think. It's hard to tell." Emerson covered her face and wavered. Reggie reached over and caught her.

"Don't push yourself." Reggie glanced to Teal. "Think they'll be waiting for us by the shuttle?"

"Not too close. The automated defenses would keep the roof clear. Probably adjacent buildings."

Emerson straightened. "Wait. They're—"

The outer wall exploded inward. Reggie dragged Emerson behind an old dryer. Through the dust, he saw a ragged hole in the wall, just over two metres across.

"Run!" Helping Emerson to her feet, he followed Teal back out the door, down a hallway, and out into the alley behind the building. The space was narrow and long, jiggering back and forth where neighbouring buildings of different sizes met—continuing the alley. Reggie couldn't make out what was on the far end through the shifting passage.

"Damn it," Teal said. "It's like being back in the basement." She shuffled sideways towards the end of the alley.

Reggie slid into the space and switched his pistol to his other hand to cover their retreat. He caught the flash of red as a gang member peeked out the door. He fired, missing, and cursed. "Go, go, go. They're behind us."

The red figure leaned into the alley again, firing off a shot from a revolver. The big slug hit the wall where Reggie had been a moment before, chipping away the stone and concrete.

They scrambled around the first obstruction and Reggie fired the next time the man popped into view. "I can't keep this up."

"It's not far." Teal held her gun out, waiting for someone coming from the other direction. She squeezed around a sharp corner that doubled back at the next buildings. "I can see the end."

Reggie sucked in and shoved himself through the tight turn and saw Teal nearing the mouth of the alley.

She slipped into the open space. "Clear."

Emerson followed. Reggie made it to the end

when the man with the revolver leaned around the corner and shot at him again. Gritting his teeth, Reggie tensed, waiting for the bullet to hit. He was tugged forward by Teal and Emerson and fell out of the narrow alley—the bullet sailing over their heads. He scrambled to his feet and they joined the commotion of a market set up in a wider thoroughfare.

THE NEON HEART

THIRTY ONE
MAD DASH

"This way." Teal ran through the crowd, avoiding the stalls. There was no coverage overhead, making the street feel like a ravine with the buildings flanking them like steep walls. People were everywhere, clogging their way. The road was speckled with hovels, booths, items for sale spread on old blankets, and vendors shoving goods in their faces. People were crammed into every corner and bunched up in front of the shops, yelling over each other. Reggie could smell food mixed with dirty people and refuse and his stomach did a somersault. He blocked out the noise and the smells and focused on staying ahead of the gang.

Teal led them through the rabble, knocking into people and kicking things cluttering the ground. "Out of the way!"

Reggie spotted flashes of red overhead on the

balconies and roofs. "They're on us." He grabbed Emerson by the shoulders and stopped her from walking into one of their lines of fire. One of them shot, the bullet hitting to the left of the Esper.

People panicked, screaming and running in all directions, turning the regular chaos into pandemonium. The Red Gang thugs overhead fired into the crowd indiscriminately, as if hoping to hit one of them by luck.

Crouching, Reggie pulled Emerson with him. "Keep your head down and follow me." He stayed as low as he could, his legs throbbing, and pushed his way through the crowd.

"I found an exit," Teal said over the comm. "I can't see you."

"Where. We'll find you." Reggie felt a body drop next to him and made sure Emerson was still behind him.

"There's an open door at the top of a stoop. Left side, yellow-brown brick."

Reggie stopped and peered through the crowd. "Got it." He led Emerson, jostled and battered by the panicking people.

They made it to the stoop and ran up the stairs. Teal had the door open and slammed it shut behind them. "I've got a bead on the shuttle. Come on."

She led them up a set of stairs. Reggie spotted a group of red clad goons on a landing above them and shot before they noticed him. The group scattered and Teal abandoned the stairs, running down the nearest hallway. Reggie followed, checking behind them for pursuit. At the end of the hall, Teal climbed out the window onto a fire escape and went up.

Reggie spotted Red Gang members on their tail as he climbed out after Emerson. "They're close."

They ran up the stairs, the metal clanging with their footfalls. Teal fired above them with a spray of bullets. A red-clad body tumbled past them, bouncing off a railing with a crunch.

They stopped before reaching the roof. Teal peeked over the top of the building, drawing a shout. "Got two of them here."

Reggie heard more shouts below them and spotted their pursuers climbing onto the fire escape. He shot down at them, making one of them dive back inside. The ones still outside returned fire. Bullets and buckshot ricocheted off the metal stairs and grates.

"Rock and a hard place," Reggie said.

"I'm on it." Teal jumped onto the roof, shooting. Reggie heard the click of her gun as she ran out of ammo, and her shout as she charged at the Reds.

He climbed onto the roof and ran after her, Emerson following. Teal was already at the first thug, pulling his own knife off his belt and plunging it into his neck and using his body as a shield. Reggie shot the other man and Teal let her shield drop.

"Over there." She pointed to a building rising over its neighbours. The roof was expanded with makeshift walls of wood, stone, and concrete. "That's our landing pad."

Reggie recognized the platform capping the roof. "What's that, like two hundred metres? How do we get there?"

Teal went to the edge. "Got a walkway half a level down. That takes us across the street. We hop the next three roofs to get to our building, then high-tail it up to the landing pad."

They heard the sounds of gang members clambering up the fire escape behind them.

"Works for me." Reggie watched Teal scoop up a rifle from the Red she'd stabbed and jump down to the bridge. It shook and swayed as she landed. He lowered Emerson down, and sat on the edge. Teal was most of the way across when the thugs chasing them crested the roof. Reggie shot the first one and dropped over the side. He landed, hoping to roll, but fell forward, opening more of the wounds from the insects, and crumpled. Wincing, he scrambled to his feet and ran across the bridge.

Teal stopped on the far side, covering him. She shot over his head, but he kept looking forward, trudging as fast as he could. He spotted a woman on the opposite roof with red spiked hair and dirty red clothes. She aimed down at Teal with a crossbow. Reggie shot at her, causing the bolt to go wide.

Teal turned and shot the woman before she could reload. Reggie stopped next to her and turned to take over covering their retreat. The goons following them had stayed behind the roofline—hiding from Teal.

She climbed up to the next roof, stopping to help Emerson. Reggie spotted a thug taking aim but shot first. The man ducked out of the way and changed his target. Reggie shot again, but the pistol clicked uselessly. He dropped the gun and stared at the man, waiting for the bullet to rip towards him.

Reggie heard a shot from above him and the man dropped. He looked up and saw Teal crouching at the edge of the roof, the rifle trained at the oncoming Reds.

"I've got you covered. Come on."

Reggie stepped on a railing and climbed next to her. He grabbed the crossbow from the dead woman and reloaded it. It had a cartridge of bolts set into the bottom that automatically slid one into place when he pulled back on the lever.

Teal fired again. "I've got our back."

Reggie nodded and ran across the roof. He sprinted the best he could with his chewed-up legs and launched himself over the gap to the next building—clearing the open space with half a metre to spare. He brought up the crossbow and scanned the surface. The only things on the roof were two rows of old air conditioner units humming loudly. He ran to check behind them and went back to the edge. "Clear."

He covered Teal and Emerson as they charged towards him. A red gang thug on the first roof stood. Reggie shot the crossbow, hoping to get close enough to drive the man back. The bolt whizzed through the air with an audible whistle and plunged into the goon's shoulder. The man yelped and grabbed at it.

Teal hopped across and slid to a stop, ready to catch Emerson. "Did you actually hit him?"

"Yeah." Reggie furrowed his brow and reloaded.

"That's crazy."

The Esper made the leap and kept running. Teal turned and ran after her. Reggie heard them grunt as they jumped to the next roof.

Reggie turned to follow them and saw a thug burst out of a roof access door. Teal shot him in midair and landed without stopping. She went to the door and continued inside. A moment later, she burst back out. "More coming this way!"

Reggie joined her on the second building and made his way to the next one. "Cover, I'll set up there." He saw Teal duck behind the small brick enclosure for the stairwell and shot at the Reds on their trail.

Emerson was already at the next roof. Reggie landed heavily next to her and dropped to a knee.

"It's clear. So is the next building, with the landing pad." The Esper helped him up.

"You read that?" Reggie turned to cover Teal. "Clear!"

Teal spun away from the enclosure and gracefully jumped over to them. "I could hear them in the stairwell."

"No time to waste." Reggie grimaced and started to jog across the empty roof. "We're almost there."

THE NEON HEART

THIRTY TWO
GOOD RIDDANCE

The original roof of the building with the landing pad was the same height as the one they were on. The extended portion made of scavenged material rose from there and covered only half the roof. The jump was farther than the other ones but Reggie didn't hesitate. His legs clattered against the side of the building as he grabbed hold. He screamed and pulled himself up.

"Emerson. You have to—" Getting to his knees, he turned and saw the Esper in mid jump. He dropped the crossbow and reached out for her, grabbing her hand. She hit the side of the building hard and lost her grip. Reggie clung to her jacket and tried to pull her up.

Teal landed next to him and got onto her belly, helping him get the girl onto the roof.

"So many on the way," she said.

They rolled away from the edge and Teal helped a dazed Emerson stand.

Reggie scooped up the crossbow and they ran for a window. He watched Red Gang members pour from the stairwell two buildings away. They joined the ones who had been in pursuit and like a ragged wave, jumped onto the adjacent roof. A dozen of them fired as soon as they landed.

Reggie took a slug in the shoulder as he and Teal shoved Emerson into the window. His jacket stopped the bullet, along with two others across his back, but the wind was knocked out of him and his arm went numb. He pushed Teal to go in next, firing behind him with the single-shot crossbow.

She slipped in easily, the glass above her shattering from a wild shot.

Reggie got hit in the leg and slumped. More shots from various weapons peppered the wall around him. Teal grabbed his jacket and pulled him inside. They crawled down the hallway, keeping under the now obliterated window, and made it to the wood board stairwell. Emerson clattered up ahead of them and Teal helped Reggie climb the awkward steps.

They reached the door to the roof and heard shooting.

"No." Reggie sighed. "We're so close."

"It's okay." Teal took his face in her hands. "It's

the turrets." She let go and pushed the door open. The heavy gun set on the platform closest to the attacking Red Gang was firing over the side of the building in a pounding rhythmic blast.

The shuttle was in the middle of the platform where they left it. As Teal approached it, the door opened.

Reggie limped to the platform. His thigh burned where he was shot. Blood oozed from the wound in slow, thick pulses. Clenching his teeth, he made it to the shuttle. Emerson stood on the ramp with her eyes closed. It shuddered as Reggie stepped onto it and she blinked.

"I was just making sure they weren't—" The Esper saw him struggle and rushed over to him. "Oh, no. You're hurt."

Reggie let her put his arm over her shoulder and help him into the shuttle. "It's not bad. I can take care of it with what's on the ship." He collapsed into the nearest seat and Emerson ran to get the first aid kit.

"Everyone in?" Teal looked back from the pilot's chair.

"Yeah." Reggie grunted as he shifted his weight. "Button us up."

Teal hit a button over her head and the ramp closed into place. "We're good, see. We made it."

Reggie checked his comm-band. There was

forty-five minutes left on the countdown. He sighed. "We're cutting it close."

Emerson returned with the medical supplies. He took the case and opened it on the seat next to him. "Thanks. You'd better buckle in."

Digging through the kit, Reggie pulled out a pair of disposable forceps, disinfectant, and bandages.

Emerson hesitated.

"It's okay. I've got this." Reggie could feel sweat bead on his forehead. "Take the copilot seat next to Teal."

Emerson nodded and shuffled off as the engines started to whine.

Reggie took out a splint and bit down on it as he jammed the forceps into his leg and dug out the bullet. He whimpered, but managed to get it on his first try.

"What's going on back there?" Teal rushed through the flight checks and clearance.

Letting the splint drop out of his mouth, Reggie grabbed the disinfectant spray. "Got hit in the thigh. Just cleaning it up. Get us out of here, please." He grimaced and coated the wound with the sticky antiseptic then wrapped up his leg in the bandages.

"We're going to make it. Don't worry." The shuttle lifted off the pad and angled towards the rest of the huge metropolis. It jolted forward as Teal punched the throttle. Reggie nearly slid out of his seat, grabbing onto the nearest rail for support. When the inertia caught up with the speed, Reggie limped up to the front of the ship.

"How's the leg?" Teal slipped into traffic, zigzagging through the slower planetary crafts.

"I'll live." Reggie clung to the back of the copilot's seat. He connected his contact lenses to the shuttle's external cameras and watched the Wall slip away behind them. The scar that ran across the city seemed harmless as they left it behind.

Reggie put his hand on Emerson's shoulder. "How are you?"

She shook her head. "I'm... okay."

Teal glanced over to her. "You will be. This was a tough one, lots of hard losses, but it gets better."

"I'm just glad I'll be able to bring my family to the space station now." Emerson looked away, likely at something projected by her implant that only she could see.

The shuttle rose above the buildings as they climbed away from the planet. Teal looked back at Reggie.

"Strap in. It's going to get rough as we break the atmosphere." She glanced at his jacket and grinned at him.

"What?" Reggie looked down. His colour-changing jacket was blood red. "Shit."

"You look like hell. Go sit."

Reggie nodded and went back to the seats lining the back cabin. He strapped into the closest one and set his lenses to show him the view from the front of the ship. The shuttle shook as the atmosphere bled into space. He saw the large bulk of the Amcoral space station spinning in high orbit, he zoomed in his view to the tiny speck that was the shipyards orbiting next to it.

The second Goliath was still there, but the framework around it had been stripped away.

"You see that?" Teal said. "It's still there. We're going to make it!"

"There's only half-an-hour left, Teal."

"We're practically there. Plenty of time!"

Out Now

Broadcast

Wasteland

ACKNOWLEDGEMENTS

This being my fourth book, you'd thing I'd have gotten the hang of it by now. Thankfully, I had a group of amazing people who were willing to give me a hand and help make it something of which I am very proud.

Christian Laforet, cofounder of Adventure Worlds Press, and my brother in literary arms not only helped me with brainstorming, editing, and design, but he came to my rescue and created the fantastic cover for this book. I hope I am half as helpful to him.

My parents have been my biggest fans and the foundation for everything I've been able to achieve in my life. I owe them for everything I am.

Alongside them are my brothers and my nephew. We are all made up of the things we admire in others. Most of the best of me is from them. The rest of the good stuff is from the people I'm lucky to call friends. Even when I was just talking about writing, they showed me unending patience and encouragement.

Several very clever, creative, and kind folks gave me reviews, edits, and beta reads. Any mistake you find likely came from my making a change after they all painstakingly went through it for me and represents the hundreds of typos, inconsistencies, plot holes, and instance of poor grammar that they did catch.

Thanks to my mum, my brother Jake, Christian Laforet, Sephorah Pohjola, Brittni Brinn, Mick Ridgewell, James Martin, Melissa Schnarr-Rice, and the good folks at Write on Windsor.

I would also like to thank the owners and staff of Anchor Coffee House for once again putting up with me sitting at the counter, writing most of this story, and chatting their ears off. Their good nature and coffee helped me make it to the end. Also, thanks to Elly Blake for joining me in the wild for writing sessions, conversation, and encouragement. She has been a natural addition to my writing friends and an inspiration.

Ben Van Dongen was born in Windsor Ontario. He likes to think that if he tried harder he could have been an Astronaut, but he is happier writing science fiction anyway. He wrote the novella The Thinking Machine, co-authored the books No Light Tomorrow and All These Crooked Streets, and is one half of the founding team of Adventure Worlds Press. You can read more crazy notions on his website. **BenVanDongen.com**

Photo by Khoa Nguyen

ADVENTUREWORLDSPRESS.COM

More Books by the Author

The Synthetic Albatross Series

The Earth Books
The Thinking Machine
The Neon Heart
Break/Interrupt

The Offworld Books
Broadcast Wasteland

Anthologies
No Light Tomorrow
All These Crooked Streets

www.ingramcontent.com/pod-product-compliance
Lightning Source LLC
Chambersburg PA
CBHW031233120726
47905CB00002B/578